POWERFUL GIRLS

A YA SHORT STORY COLLECTION

DAYLE A. DERMATIS

SOUL'S
ROAD
PRESS

ABOUT THIS BOOK

All girls have power. Sometimes magic, sometimes bravery, sometimes sheer determination.

In this collection, teenage girls face their fears, trust their instincts, and protect those around them....

And in the process, learn more about themselves and grow closer to the powerful women they will become.

Featuring a Tangent Online *2018 Recommended Read and an excerpt of the novel* Beautiful Beast, *this collection will enchant and empower readers of any age.*

"...an entertaining journey."

– *Tangent Online,* "Family Fair and True,"
2018 Recommended Reading List

*D*on't worry," the Lawrence Prep school administrator assured my aunt and uncle. "We think Zoey has great potential."

My gaze snapped from the glorious view of the sun-drenched Pacific out the massive picture window over her shoulder to the administrator herself. They think *what*, now?

I glanced at Aunt Bonnie and Uncle Dave. Their expressions mirrored the face I was pretty sure I was making. Only for different reasons.

They hoped, but didn't really think, I had potential. They didn't know I'd overheard them when I was packing to come to the school, when she said quietly to him, "This is Zoey's last chance," and he said, "Let's just hope she doesn't screw this one up, too," and she said, "Or worse."

I, on the other hand, thought I did have potential, but I didn't believe the administrator when she said that. Once bitten, and all that.

My best guess was that Aunt Bonnie and Uncle Dave had spent a lot of money to get me into Lawrence Prep, and that pleased the administrator, who needed to keep admissions up so she could preserve her flawless complexion when she hit the far side of thirty. She was pretty in a cool blond way, but to my surprise, when she smiled, she looked like she really meant it.

And she smiled when she said the school thought I had great potential.

I hugged my aunt and uncle good-bye, and honestly, I *was* grateful for everything and I *was* going to miss them, because they were practically all I had left in the world family-wise.

Their leaving made me feel, all emotionally and irrationally, that I was an orphan all over again.

They'd done their best, for a couple who'd chosen to be child-free and then agreed to take in their teenaged niece after her mother had been killed in Afghanistan and her father had chosen the sweet breath of carbon monoxide rather than life without his wife.

It wasn't their fault I'd been kicked out of school.

If you're going to blame anyone for that, blame my therapist. Or maybe the school, for not understanding art, or something.

I've loved art ever since my fat fingers could hold onto those fat kid-sized crayons. Colors, lines, shapes…I eschewed coloring books for my own designs, even if nobody but me could identify them. I graduated to colored pencils, watercolors, pastels, and finally delicious, expressive oils.

Once, my parents had taken me on vacation to Breckenridge, Colorado, up in the mountains where the air was thin. There was something dangerously glorious about it, about every breath being so pure and important, and that dizzy wonder was how painting, and art, felt to me.

Now, if I kept my head down and graduated high school, I could figure out how to make painting my life.

Right now, though, the administrator—Ms. Benz—took me on a tour of the campus, pointing out the gym, the dining hall, the class buildings.

The buildings were modern, with lots of glass to let in the southern California light and afford views of the ocean and mountains. The dorm buildings were strange, though. Instead of being flat, next to every window there was a bump, like half of a tower, sticking out. The towers were also mostly glass.

My room was on the top floor, facing the Pacific. I wondered if they'd put me there because the view was supposed to be calming. I knew I would have a roommate, but hadn't heard anything about her; the spot had opened up here, and my aunt and uncle had jumped on the chance, and boom, here I was.

I admit my jaw dropped when I saw the room.

It wasn't huge—I guess it was average by dorm room standards—but the view was, in fact, spectacular. My roommate's side of the room was cluttered and decorated with a lot of pale pink, which I mostly forgave because I saw toe shoes dangling from a hook on the wall. Pink came with the territory.

My side was a blank slate: metal twin bed with white sheets and a dark blue fuzzy blanket, simple wooden desk with a wooden bookshelf next to it, a dresser, and louvered doors to a closet.

We'd bump into each other when we both tried to see in the mirror over the sink, but otherwise, we'd be fine unless we ended up loathing each other.

Whatever. We'd work it out. All I cared about was the half-tower annex on my side of the room.

It was, as it looked from the outside, a half-moon room made of glass. It was mostly empty, except for a long wooden table…and an easel.

On my roomie's side, her annex was mostly empty, too. But I saw a barre along the inner wall, and speakers where you could hook up an iPod.

Artist spaces.

I whirled on Ms. Benz. "Really? Thi...?" I sounded like a dork, but in my exhilaration I didn't care.

She smiled, still looking enthusiastic. "Lawrence Prep encourages its students to follow their passions and excel in the field of their choice. You'll be expected to keep up your grades in all subjects, of course, but as a private school we have a flexible curriculum, which means you'll be able to focus on what you do best.

"In your case, as I understand it, that would be painting."

My stomach flip-flopped. "Have you...seen my work?"

She shook her head. Her silky blond hair swung with the movement. "I'm no expert, I'm afraid. It was Mr. Waters, the head of the art department, who argued that your artwork made you an excellent candidate for Lawrence Prep."

I didn't know what had happened to the painting that had gotten me expelled. I assumed it was gone forever, along with the rest of them.

After Ms. Benz left, I lost myself lost in a frenzy of unpacking. Clothes I threw in the dresser or closet, along with my half-empty suitcase. I did take the time to charge my laptop and phone, and to set out one more important thing: A digital photo frame.

I didn't turn it on yet; I wasn't ready to see the pictures of my parents (and a few of my grandparents, and Aunt Bonnie and Uncle Dave, and some friends) just yet. Just having the frame there was enough right now.

I dug into my backpack and pulled out a brass WWII lighter. I wasn't sure if lighters were allowed here, but this one was important. My mom had carried it with her—although she hadn't taken it to the Middle East—and after she died, her father somehow got it, and gave it to me.

It had been my great-grandfather's, and had been passed down the line. Supposedly it had allowed him to build a fire on a night so cold he wouldn't have made it through otherwise.

"Only use it for something really important, Zoey," my grandfather had said.

I tucked the lighter behind the picture frame and turned my attention to the most important thing I needed to do.

My workspace called to me.

Paints, brushes, palettes went on the table. Large sketch books and painting paper I stacked underneath. I had only a few canvases, which I propped in a corner, and wondered if they'd supply me with more.

Clearly they were more than okay with me painting. Whether they'd be okay with the subject matter remained to be seen.

Once again, emotions bubbled up inside of me, making my jaw clench and my hands fist and my heart race. Grief. Anger at my father for giving up. Loneliness and abandonment.

My fingers ached to hold a brush; my heart ached to release the churning feelings onto the canvas. When I painted from my gut like that (which, I suppose, I'd always done, but the therapist had specifically suggested I paint how I felt *about my parents*), it felt as though I transferred those emotions onto the canvas. I released them, and it...helped.

I would still be angry and sad, but I would no longer feel overwhelmed by uncontrollable anger and sadness.

I was reaching for a palette when the door burst open and I got my first view of my roommate. She was tiny, but seemed to be all limbs and movement and energy until she saw me, at which point she stopped briefly.

"Hi! You must be Zoey. I'm your roomie, Shannon Szabó."

She had a triangular, almost fox-like face. The vulpine look was accentuated by her enormous dark eyes and the way she pulled her thick dark hair back into two buns on top of her head.

I felt the urge to paint her, a fox-maiden wearing a scarlet cape like Little Red Riding Hood, huge liquid eyes forward and trusting...while behind her a wolf loomed, mouth gaping, all yellowed teeth and lolling tongue...

I shook my head. Where had *that* image come from? I usually didn't know what I wanted to paint until I had my brush in hand.

As much as my hand did itch to hold a brush again, and as much as Lawrence Prep apparently supported that idea, I now knew to hide anything that might be misinterpreted as me wanting to commit a major felony.

I didn't want that. I'd never even *thought* that.

A year ago, if you'd asked me what I wanted, I would've said I wanted to make a living doing art. I didn't necessarily need to be famous, but I wanted to be selling, to be respected for what I did, to have people like and buy my work.

Six months ago, I would've said I wanted my parents back.

Now...both, and yet...

I shook my head again. Now I wanted to get through this, get my degree and make it to eighteen so I could go back to my dream of being an artist. Until then, I'd have to hide whatever work I did that wasn't acceptable to Lawrence Prep or polite society or the NSA.

"So, the rumor is you tried to burn down your last school

or something," Shannon said with undisguised enthusiasm, drifting down onto her bed and curling into a lotus pose as if she were a leaf on the wind.

Fuck. How had *that* rumor gotten started, much less made its way here?

"No," I said. "Not even remotely. I'm just a misunderstood *arteeste*."

She snorted. "Okay, well, as long as you don't try to murder me in my sleep, we're copacetic."

I was pretty sure *copacetic* meant *good*. I hoped so.

"No, although sometimes my artwork can be a little graphic," I said. "It doesn't represent what I want to happen, though. It's just…art. It's what it needs to be."

She nodded. "No, I totally get that. Sometimes when I dance, I don't care about the steps or being technically right —I dance how I feel. Before, I was marked down for that. But here, they encourage it."

"Did I miss much before I got here?" I asked.

She shrugged, able to make even that simple movement a graceful statement. "Meeting teachers, getting books…if you've got half a brain, you can catch up. And don't worry about the rest of us. Everyone's been dying to meet you— although they'll probably be disappointed you didn't try to burn anything down."

I learned a lot, my first weeks at Lawrence Prep.

I learned how to get lost, then learned how to find my way around—especially where the art building was. I learned I didn't entirely suck at volleyball, which was good because we were all required to do some sport, even if that sport was yoga.

I learned that while I did disappoint the students who

hoped I'd be a fascinating firebug, I was still accepted, and along with Shannon, I had friends.

And I learned that something was just not quite right about the seemingly idyllic Lawrence Prep.

It took about a week and a half for my new social circle to ask me about the setting-the-school-on-fire rumor. We were sprawled on the big sloping lawn overlooking the ocean, and we were supposed to be studying.

But Todd was trying to explain to Alma about time travel in *Doctor Who* (Todd was a science nerd anyway, whereas Alma was into botany—apparently she'd assisted her parents when they'd catalogued a rare species of orchid in the Ecuadorian Amazon), and Bharat was using his binoculars either to ID birds for a class or spy on students in the dorms (although the glass was treated, so he couldn't see a damn thing).

He was also smoking weed, which he insisted was for medicinal purposes, but in his world, "medicinal" meant "expanding my mind so I can write the next great work of literature." Whatevs.

Me, I was just lying on the grass, glad that we had enough ocean breezes to counteract the hot, dry Santa Ana winds, and pondering my next painting.

Typical of Southern California, there wasn't a cloud in the sky. I'd moved around because of my mom being in the military, and the relentless pale blue and inescapable sun here gave me a sense of near-agoraphobia sometimes. Thankfully, now wasn't one of those times.

I had more to be worrying about.

I'd started having nightmares about my father's death—

thankfully Shannon was a deep sleeper, because I was waking up in the middle of the night and prowling the room for something, anything, to calm me down—and I knew that before the anger and grief took complete hold, I had to paint them out.

In my mind was forming an idea that was gruesome and satisfying, and I worried how Mr. Waters would react to it.

Now, Shannon—who had been twirling to music only she could hear—dropped gracefully onto the prickly grass next to me.

Her joining us interrupted everyone else, and after we chatted for a bit, it was Bharat who finally broached the question.

"So, what *did* you do to get expelled?" he asked, his brown face scrunched up as if he'd been pondering a deep problem.

I sighed. Might as well. It wasn't nearly as bad as arson.

Just more personal.

"After my parents died, I was pretty messed up," I said, fighting back emotions and keeping my voice light. "My therapist..."

Everyone nodded. Oh, right, Hollyweird, where therapy was as much a part of growing up as getting training wheels taken off your bike.

"When my therapist found out I was an artist, he told me to express my feelings that way. So I did. And it helped. The paintings were just for me, but I thought one of them was pretty good, and I was behind on projects for art class at school, so I took it in."

"You got expelled for taking art to school?" Alma's voice registered her disbelief.

You can't describe abstract art—saying "there was lots of red to symbolize blood and guns because my mother was a soldier and a truck blown apart because that's what happened to her and…"—makes you sound like an idiot and your artwork sound like crap.

So I said, "There were guns in it, and bomb fragments, and the school had a zero tolerance policy when it came to suggestions of terrorism. They basically decided that the painting meant I was going to come to school, mow everyone down, and then blow the place up."

Because they were idiots.

"That's idiotic," Bharat said.

"*Thank* you," I said, throwing up my hands.

"Didn't your therapist explain?" Shannon asked, putting her feet flat together, her knees on the ground, and leaning forward into the stretch while still looking at me. She could never keep still. It should have been annoying, but it was somehow comforting. Maybe because I was always in my own head.

I snorted. "The dickhead refused on grounds of doctor-patient confidentiality. Which mean, of course, that *he* didn't think I was dangerous, because if he had, that would've superseded confidentiality and he would've had to report it. Besides, zero tolerance, remember?"

I didn't want to get into the other paintings, which I figured I'd never see again. Despite what they'd represented, they'd been my best work.

And my last tie to my parents.

I could paint more. I *would* paint more.

"Don't get kicked out of here," Alma said earnestly. The others nodded.

"I'll do my best not to," I said. "But art is art, you know?"

Shannon knew, and maybe Bharat did. I wasn't sure if the others did, but they nodded again.

I got up and walked to the end of the slope, looking out over the glittering water. I had to start painting again.

Oh, I'd done some smaller works, but I was holding back. I was scared, I knew it. Scared of being told *no*, scared of losing this last chance, scared of my own emotions.

Ergo, nightmares.

Either I was going to paint, or I really was going to do something I—and the school—would regret.

I had the usual junior classes to deal with: AP English, Chemistry, US History, Spanish 3, Sociology. The school really did let me focus on art, though, and for that I was in awe.

Mr. Waters didn't say what artwork of mine he had seen —telling someone "This is your best work" could be as devastating as telling them what was wrong with it, he said.

The first time I met with him, I perched on a tall metal stool behind a paint-and-ink-stained art table, trying to find a comfortable way to hook my feet on the rungs without becoming a pretzel.

Mr. Waters sat across from me, viewing copies of my art on an iPad. The swish of his finger to flip between photos was almost hypnotic. He wasn't terribly tall, and although his hair was dark, his goatee had started to grey.

"Your work is good," he said. His pale blue eyes blinked rapidly, a tic I was already getting used to. "Really good. My job is to encourage you to make your work phenomenal. You have *so* much potential, Zoey. I can't wait to see what you're going to do with it."

In very great hindsight, he might have said "what *we're* going to do with it." Which, in very great hindsight, makes a lot of sense.

At the time, though, I heard what I needed to hear. He said my work was phenomenal, and I had potential.

❀

Mr. Waters assigned a senior, Matty Lui, to be my student mentor. Matty had been at Lawrence Prep since her freshman year. She showed me around the art building, helped me get the supplies I needed, and encouraged me, as Mr. Waters had, to follow my passion, my heart.

I hadn't told either of them that my heart was angry and sad, that those emotions drove my painting.

Matty herself was my first indication that something was rotten in the State of Denmark (thank you, AP English). Mr. Waters called her his prize pupil, someone he himself had been mentoring.

But he didn't say she had great potential. He said "She does very good work. I'm quite proud of her."

I'm far from perfect, and I'm not going to say I'm a total expert on art, but Matty's work—the stuff I saw, her recent work—was technically fine, but…passionless. Soulless. She did lovely, competent, will-have-a-decent-career work.

And then there was Matty herself. She was friendly, help-ful, not quite my bestie but always saying the right thing. She seemed…tired. Worn out. A shell of who she was before—and I made a point of finding out who she was before.

First I Googled her, of course. Found the *Ventura County Star* article about her winning a California-wide art contest when she was in the eighth grade. The picture was a cute younger version of the Matty I knew: long black hair, Asian eyes, high cheekbones dusted with freckles (okay, the grainy newspaper picture didn't show the freckles), big grin.

She didn't grin as much now, but I saw the young Matty in the ghost of her current smile.

I found out where her room was, and made up some lame excuse to seek her out one Saturday night. She was in the same dorm as me, two floors down and a few rooms to the right.

Some of the doors were open, through which wafted music, laughter, and weed. I wondered if Bharat knew, then shrugged. They probably shared the same dealer.

"Have you seen my box of pastels?" I asked. "Did I leave them in the art building? I wanted to use them this weekend."

Her side of the room was the other side from mine, and decorated with a big emerald fan with Asian writing on it, multicolored Post-Its for a science project, and posters of some thrash-metal band I'd never heard of. Her roommate wasn't in. I kept rambling, wandering into her art space as I went.

"I love these rooms—so much light to paint by," I continued. "Oh, hey, is this some of your stuff I haven't seen?" I was already pulling out the canvases, flipping to the furthest-back ones stacked on the floor under the assumption that they'd be the oldest ones.

"Hey," she said, hand on my arm. "Stop it. That's not… that's *rude*, Zoey."

But I'd already seen what I needed to see. Even after I'd mumbled my sorries and gotta gos and thanks for the advices, the painting followed me.

An Asian dragon, cobalt blue with flecks of gold—mixed media, because the gold really sparkled. Its eyes had locked onto mine, I swear. I felt as though I could hear its roar in my mind, feel its hot breath on my back as I beat my retreat down the hallway.

That painting had a life that none of her current work had. What I saw in it was passion and drive and, well, potential for greatness (in my oh-so-humble opinion).

What had happened to her?

Or was I seeing patterns where no patterns existed?

In the meantime, I painted. I worked in art class on most projects, but my big one—the one I couldn't stop painting if I tried—I kept in my room, working mostly when Shannon was out.

Despite how accepting everyone here had been about my past work, possibly even the stuff that had gotten me expelled, I was wary of showing this one off.

Even for me, it was creepy.

My father's face, melting, surrounded by gasoline vapors through which demonic faces leered. Everything was surreal, abstract, except for a small photo of my mother—one I'd printed out on glossy paper—of her in camo, her hair pulled severely back and mostly hidden in under a cap, but despite the fact that she wasn't smiling, the dimple on her left cheek was visible.

Before we left for winter break, I draped a sheet over it; then, on a whim, painted a faint line from the sheet onto the floor. If the sheet was moved, the line wouldn't match up.

I had no idea if I was being reasonably paranoid or if I was actually going a little crazy.

Over winter break, I channeled my energy into designing handmade cards for my family and friends. Aunt Bonnie and Uncle Dave seemed more relaxed, and I figured that meant they were receiving positive reports from Lawrence Prep. I slept a lot and caught up on *Sherlock* and Instagram, and by the time I was ready to go back, I had convinced myself everything was fine.

It had been the stress of starting a new school—midsemester, no less—especially after what had happened at the last school.

Of course things had seemed off-kilter. *I* had been off-kilter.

I wasn't back more than a day before I realized I was wrong. Still paranoid or crazy; the jury was still out on that count.

Shannon and I had a squealy-huggy reunion and immediately dumped all our Christmas loot out to show each other. But as the weeks wore on, she seemed...different.

Was she moving a little less, a little slower? She didn't seem to have the dance in her step anymore.

Todd and Alma also seemed less focused. At first I chalked it up to the fact that they'd started dating; ergo, major distraction. But Alma started talking about teaching high school science instead of being an Indiana-Jones-style botanist finding new species in the jungle, and Todd spent more time watching *Doctor Who* reruns than studying.

As for Bharat, his weed smoking seemed to have taken on an edge of desperation, and he was the only one to articulate a change.

"I can't find the words," he said, a hint of desperation in his voice as he drew in the smoke. His eyes were red-rimmed. "They're...it's like they're far away, and I can't reach them anymore."

We were down a path behind a sage scrub, after dark. Winter, when the desert turns cold. I shoved my hands deeper into the pockets of my hoodie and said nothing. I didn't have any experience with artistic block.

At the same time, the teachers seemed to be extra-perky. Ms. Benz's skin glowed, looking as soft as a toddler's. Mr. Waters's goatee seemed darker, and his blinky-tic had mostly subsided.

Ms. Benz could've gotten a stellar facial, and Mr. Waters could have dyed his goatee, but I couldn't explain the tic, or their overall energy.

As for my painting, nobody had looked at it. Either they didn't know, or they didn't care.

I'd taken the lighter home with me over break. Now I kept it in my backpack, which felt safer than behind the frame.

And I started searching for an explanation.

Lawrence Prep was a fairly new school—founded only eleven years ago—so there wasn't much about its alumni. The graduates I did manage to find online all had decent jobs, but nothing spectacular. Not that everyone can be President or an Oscar-winning movie star, but still. When I looked those people up in the yearbooks in the library, as freshmen they'd all had big dreams.

Not a one of them had achieved those dreams. Not even close.

They'd lost the dreams, the hope, somewhere along the way.

What, then, had happened to all that potential?

I watched the other students. The current freshmen still seemed pretty focused, driven. The current seniors, like Matty, looked tired; they had their heads down studying in anticipation of graduation, sure, but it seemed dogged.

Was this how all schools were? Had I just not noticed it at my previous schools?

But when I saw it in myself, I knew beyond a shadow of a doubt that there was something in the air, or the water, or...*something*.

The longer the semester wore on, the less I wanted to paint, except on my personal work. Previously, as much as I'd been needing to paint to get my emotions out, I still needed to work on other things, too. Now I was doing less and less in art lab, and not caring.

The only time I felt alive again was when I was throwing my feelings into my private paintings.

I rolled up the painting of my father, and Bharat, the little criminal, produced a key to the English building. I tucked the painting behind a couple of dusty file cabinets in a storage room.

Then I started another. I'd been painting about the past, and now, this time, my gut pushed me towards a future that would never be. My mom had been working her way up through the ranks, and I painted her with lieutenant colonel silver oak leaves on her shoulders. I painted my dad, who'd loved to run, triumphant at the finish line of the New York Marathon.

My other grades were slipping—not dramatically, not enough to get me kicked out—as I spent more time trying to figure out just what the hell was going on.

At it turned out, Mr. Waters made it easy in the end.

He took me aside one day and told me he wanted to assess my progress. Which made no sense, because he had access to every piece of art I'd done so far, except for the two personal ones.

That was weird enough to confirm that Mr. Waters was definitely part of what was going on.

Dressed in black jeans and my black hoodie, I followed him one evening when he left the art building. I had two things in my pockets: my phone, in case I needed to call for help, and my lighter, for superstitious comfort.

The Santa Monica mountains were formed by earthquakes, which meant they looked like folded meringue. You had your peaks, and then your canyons, which were further eroded by the spring rains after the annuals fire that wiped out all the trees that kept the soil together.

In the canyon next to Lawrence Prep was an old military facility. From the satellite view on Google Maps, it was just a cluster of one-story cement buildings. Students were forbidden to go there, but of course some tried anyway. As far as I'd heard, no one had ever succeeded—the high, electrified fence with a roll of barbed wire at the top was a major deterrent, plus some kids said when they got there, they decided it just wasn't worth it.

We'd had spring rain, so the path wasn't completely dry, which probably helped keep my footsteps quiet. I felt my way along in the bare light of a half-full moon, hoping to hell I didn't trip.

Something—something seriously bigger than a ground squirrel—rustled in the scrub next to me, and I leapt sideways, swallowing a shriek.

Two faces, wide-eyed, stared at me. Students I didn't know. I pressed a hand to my chest as if that would contain my pounding heart. Idiots. Were they trying to get expelled?

What I was doing could get me expelled—again.

But I had to know what was going on.

I shook my head at the lovers and continued on.

When I got down into the canyon, I got a serious case of the blahs. This wasn't really worth it—it was a stupid idea— I should just go back.

But I saw Mr. Waters ease open a gate in the fence, and that spurred me on.

I certainly hoped it hadn't re-electrified after he went through. I tossed a stick at the fence and nothing happened, but he could flip a switch at any time. It took me several moments of reaching out and pulling back my hand before I had the courage to touch it, and when I did, I just snatched out and grabbed the gate.

My hair didn't frizz straight out and I didn't get flung twenty feet through the air, so that was copacetic.

My mouth dry and my nerves seriously frazzled, I eased open the heavy metal door into the first bunker in time to see Mr. Waters, at the end of the long hall, open a door on the right. So I tiptoed my way down that hall and carefully opened that door, tan metal with a frosted window.

I gagged. The air in the hallway had been dry, but this air was dry and palpably thick, and it reeked of something. Skunk and sewer, kind of.

Black iron stairs spiraled down into darkness, circling around an open space. The only faint lights were around the upper perimeter, so I couldn't see the floor below, but I could hear Mr. Waters's footsteps, and then another door opening and closing.

My move. I hurried down the steps, and as I did, the bottom of the pit came into view out of the dimness. Whatever it was heaved and oozed, a grey-green mass in which I could see curved lumps.

It was beyond creepy. I had no frame of reference. Whatever was going on was now officially freaking me out.

I was terrified. Expulsion had become the least of my worries. That heaving ooze was just not normal. What had I stumbled into—and would I get out of it?

Then I thought about my mother, her bravery. Her sacrifice. I took another step. Then another.

One floor above the bog of eternal stench, the stairs leveled out to a walkway, and I saw the door Mr. Waters had gone through.

I opened the door, just a tiny crack, and peered in.

I could see, in the crack, Mr. Waters, and Ms. Benz, and my AP English teacher and Shannon's Psychology teacher. I could tell there were more—maybe everyone from the school.

And I saw a sliver of a chart on the wall.

"Zoey Fontaine is a concern," Mr. Waters was saying. "I don't know why I'm unable to tap into her potential."

"I keep telling you not to worry about it," Ms. Benz said in her light voice. "There's enough for us, and all the children."

The chart on the wall looked like it had students' names on it. Matty's name was on top, with a line leading to something I couldn't read—not just a foreign language, but an unknown alphabet. Alma's name was a tier down, also with a line to an alien text.

"We can feed us all," Ms. Benz continued. "And when the children are born, they can start their own academies to continue the process."

Holy freaking Predator-Torchwood-Battleship. Aliens who sucked out students'…potential? and…*ate* it or something?

I must've gasped, because Shannon's Psych teacher frowned and turned towards the door.

Eeeeeeee…

I'd never been particularly athletic (volleyball notwithstanding), but now I understood adrenaline panic. I ran up the stairs two at a time, legs burning, lungs laboring in the thick, smelly air. Fear didn't let me slow down. I heard shouts behind me, but apparently they didn't have laser pistols or whatever potential-sucking aliens carried for weapons.

I yanked open the door at the top of the stairs. Looked back.

And without thinking—just feeling, *knowing*—I pulled the lighter, the metal cold against my flesh, from my pocket. Stared at it. Flicked it open, and tossed it into the void.

This important enough for you, great-grandpa?

The little flame flipped end over end, and I prayed on my parents' graves that it wouldn't go out. There were more shouts, and the door below slammed.

As the lighter reached the lowest level, the air shimmered like heat off asphalt, and then the flame hit the alien baby-sac goo, and I heard a surprisingly loud *whoosh*.

I slammed the door. Through the frosted window, it looked as though the flames reached all the way up.

I went back to running, but nobody followed me up the canyon.

I spent the night in Alma's room, just in case, although I didn't sleep.

Classes were mysteriously cancelled the next day, and the dining hall just had cereal out for breakfast, lunch, and dinner. The staff was close-lipped, just telling us to sit tight. (Apparently I hadn't killed all of them—or the cooks and servers were actually human. How would we know?) A lot of kids called home in a panic, and everyone milled about, not quite sure what to do.

I snuck my painting out of the English building closet, and sat it on my art table next to my latest one, as if they were weapons.

The day after that, the formal announcement was made that Lawrence Prep had suffered some type of financial issue and was closing, effective immediately. Our transcripts would be sent to other schools with glowing recommendations.

The last thing I packed was my latest painting. Before I rolled it up, I looked at it, hard.

I realized, then, what I'd painted.

My parents' lost potential.

It made me angry, and I didn't realize I was crying until Shannon stepped up next to me and handed me a tissue.

I honked into it, and hugged her. She already seemed a

little perkier, and I wondered if everyone was going to recover.

No, I *knew* they would—most of them, anyway.

Potential can't be sucked away if you're still alive. It's your choice to give up.

But I was still going to be wary about anyone who told me how great my potential was.

FAMILY, FAIR AND TRUE

The hawthorn, one of many trees growing in the hedgerow between two farmers' meadows, was a dark silhouette against the blue-black of the nearly midnight sky, but the three-quarter moon gave enough light to illuminate the pale scraps of cloth and other items that had been tied around its branches.

A rag tree—a wishing tree—overlooking the holy well I sought.

I was off to make a wish that would change my life forever, and even though it was what I'd wanted for as long as I could remember, my stomach fizzed with nervousness.

I tramped across the meadow, sure-footed even in the darkness. Nearly midnight on the eve of Beltane, on the eve of my sixteenth birthday. An auspicious birthday for me, because sixteen is one and six, which makes seven, and that was a magical number to the Tylwyth Teg, the Fair Family, the faerie folk of Wales.

The last night of April was always a chill one, and I stuffed my hands in the pockets of my hoodie, curling my fingers into my palms to both warm them and keep them from trembling. The long grass shushed beneath my feet, and although the air was still, every so often I caught a faint whiff of sheep.

When I reached the hawthorn and the well, I pulled out my mobile to check the time. Ten minutes to go. Just enough time.

It was called St. Mary's Well—*Fynnon Fair* in Welsh—but it had pagan roots, as most things around here did. The people who came here to worship, no matter what faith they held, kept the tree and the well tidy, and whichever farmer technically owned the hedgerow didn't mind. Or, more likely, neither of them owned it. Which made sense. It was a place between, and places between are always holy and magical. Boundaries between one thing and another, but being neither one thing nor the other.

A faint breeze caressed and fluttered the offerings on the tree. Scraps of fabric and yarn, mostly, but also a plastic bag, and what looked like a strand of faux metallic plastic beads, which clacked and clattered softly. The centuries-old tradition was that you came to the well and the tree for healing, and you tied your wish for health onto the tree, and as the fabric rotted away and disintegrated, so your affliction would fade away. Which is why the Tesco's bag and the beads made no sense.

Now people come to this tree and well for a variety of wishes, not just about health. Love, fertility, happiness, I don't know.

I doubted very few, if any, had come here to make the wish I held so deeply in my heart.

At a minute to midnight, I walked down into the well.

The stairs were uneven, worn in the center from centuries of petitioners easing down into the tight space.

Sixteen steps down into the earth. Doesn't sound like many, but it was enough that by the time I got to the bottom, my head was not only beneath the level of the stone rim, but below the roofline that covered the well itself. My shoulders almost brushed against the mossy sides of the chamber.

My feet crunched over tiny snail shells as I descended, the air growing more moist and cold, and the darkness more complete. The weak moonlight couldn't extend this far into the earth. I reached the bottom, breathing in the earthy scent of loam, and stopped.

I thought about why I was here, and what I wished for. I couldn't go on if I had any doubts, any hesitation.

But this was what I had yearned for since I was old enough to understand what I was.

A *plentyn cael*. A changeling child.

My "parents," Cerys and John (I couldn't really call them my adoptive parents, as they'd had no choice in the matter), had brought home from the hospital a sweet, fair-haired baby and then found, shortly thereafter, a temperamental, black-haired thing in the crib. (The latter would be me.)

If they had tried any of the folk remedies to banish a changeling, they refused to tell me, but I couldn't imagine that they didn't make an attempt to get their real child back. Why wouldn't they? Cerys was a professor of folklore and mythology at uni, and John was a renowned fantasy artist; they knew what had happened.

Instead, they'd passed me off as their own, despite the fact that I'm dark and thin and plain, whereas both of them are blond, both attractive; Cerys curvy, John tall.

I've seen the looks we get when we're in public together—both because I don't look anything like them, but also because I don't look *right*. People can tell there's something off about me, something otherworldly, although they can never put their finger on it. I don't have pointed ears or walk like I'm gliding. I just make people look away, their gaze sliding sideways and down.

The looks used to hurt, but I've built up a wall and taught myself not to care, reminding myself that I *am* different.

To the world, Cerys and John call me theirs. I was grateful they'd told me the truth, though.

I hadn't told them where I was going when I left tonight. They trust me. They were used to my long rambles in the woods, even this late—after all, it wasn't a school night. Perhaps they even assume that given my nature, my blood, no harm will come to me.

Now, despite my best efforts to tamp it down, guilt rose on the fizzy bubbles of nerves. I did leave them a note on my pillow.

I appreciated everything they'd done for me, I told them in the note (and it was true), and I'd been fond of them, and soon they'd have their real daughter back, and I knew they'd be happy again. I'd signed it *Thank you, Poppy.*

They had, in fact, treated me as well as if I'd been their own. They'd fed me, clothed me, nagged me to get good grades, encouraged me to explore what inspired me, hugged me, included me.

But they'd done all that out of duty, not out of love. They accepted the burden of raising a child not their own, when their own had been taken.

They were not my parents, and for as long as I've had memory, I've wanted to find my real parents. The Tylwyth Teg, the faeries who exchanged me for another.

And so I'd come here to wish, and perform a ritual that should lead me to my true home.

I crouched down and swiped on my mobile's flashlight. My fingers shook, not from the cold, but from the realization that I was finally *here*, it was going to happen *now*, if I did everything correctly. *Please oh please...*

The stone-bordered rectangular pool of the well extended about a third of a meter back and was twice as wide. The water came from a natural spring deep in the earth, and looked darker than the midnight around me.

In the niche behind it were the melted wax remains of candles, as well as rough-hewn crosses made from two sticks and bits of twine, dried brown flowers, a tiny corn dolly propped up in the corner, and a scattering of small polished rocks, shells, and coins.

Whooshing out a nervous breath, I pulled out of my pocket my own, delicate offering: a whisper-thin braided strand of three of my own hairs. The fae admire difficult tasks completed.

Bracing myself against the ceiling with one hand, I tucked the braid-wisp into the niche. Then I stretched down to scoop some water into my hand.

I pulled three palmfuls of water into my mouth, and held them there. The water tasted of copper and was shockingly cold, making my teeth and the bones of my hand ache.

I eased myself into a turn, no simple feat in the tight space, and ascended. My boot caught on one of the uneven stone steps and I almost swallowed the water in my mouth before I caught myself, my hands scraping against the rough, cold rock of the stairs above me.

Once I reached the top, I stepped around the well opening three times in a clockwise direction, ending up at the head of the well in front of the bushy hawthorn. It was too early for its white flowers to bloom; now there were only dark, waxy leaves and the ever-present thorns.

From my pocket I drew an inch-wide strip of fine, oyster-white silk, a piece of the cloth I'd been swaddled in when Cerys and John found me in their baby's crib.

As I knotted the silk on the tree, I visualized my wish: to be reunited with my true parents, whoever they were. Rich or poor, noble or peasant or however it worked there. To go *home*.

With a surprising prick of tears in my eyes, I thought of the centuries-old cottage I lived in with Cerys and John, of my bedroom, cozy thanks to the foot-thick, whitewashed stone walls. Of the kitchen that smelled like oregano and basil and garlic because John loved to cook Italian food (I hoped faerie food tasted half as good); of the messy study crammed full of papers and stacks of Cerys's research books, her laptop precariously balanced on one pile, where I'd loved to play as a child, warm and safe.

It was all I'd ever known as a home, and I hadn't expected to miss it—and them.

I felt a sudden bump in my throat, but still didn't swallow. I banished those memories.

That home had been temporary. What I needed, desperately, was to learn what my real home was and who my real family was.

And so I channeled all my energy and visions and thoughts into my wish as I gave the silk to the hawthorn.

It was only then I realized the legends and instructions never specified what I was supposed to do with the water in my mouth. Spitting it out seemed to defeat the purpose somehow, if not being outright rude. I shrugged. If this didn't work, I'd probably contract dysentery or some equally hideous plague.

But I believed it *would* work, so I swallowed the coppery-tasting water, still icy cold. I'd almost become used to the bitterness by now, but my tongue was numb.

No magic comes without sacrifice, right?

I did so just as my mobile's alarm chimed softly to tell me it was midnight, and just as a pure white light flashed from the well.

My stomach lurched—either from terror/disbelief/relief or from the cold water landing in it—and my heart pounded in my throat. In a few steps I was around to the entrance.

The light had faded to a glow, strong enough that I couldn't see the pool below any more than I had been able to see it in the dark.

It was obvious that I should go down again. My wish was being granted, and I shouldn't waste any time.

I descended carefully, mindful of how I'd tripped on the way up, and how my legs felt weak and shaky. I felt for the edge of each step before I committed to it, because I couldn't see the worn rock.

I counted as I went, pausing when I hit sixteen steps. Previously, the next step I took would have landed my foot in the pool of the well. Then I continued, and touched another step, and another, and another, down into the earth towards the source of the light.

It was happening. I pressed a hand to my mouth, not sure whether I felt like laughing or crying. *It was really happening.*

The light changed as I went further down, from white to the blueish-purple of twilight—the time of day when the barrier between the worlds was thinnest—to a gentle gold of lamplight and the birth of new days.

The steps ended and opened onto a vast, luxurious, cavernlike space.

Bloody hell. I was finally here. The breath whooshed out of me and for a moment I couldn't make my legs move me forward.

It had worked.

I was here.

I was home.

I was overwhelmed.

Painted silk tapestries in watery colors of pearl grey and blues and greens, glinting with stitches of gold, hung from ornate rods. The light came not only from pierced silver lanterns but some ambient source I couldn't find.

The ceiling soared into darkness, so high I couldn't see

where it ended, but occasionally I thought I glimpsed the sparkle of some flying thing, swooping and dipping.

The air was soft against my skin, and I felt light, as if gravity had less of a hold here. Floating on the air came the chink of glasses, murmurs of voices, soft swells of laughter. There was music, too, but I couldn't tell where it came from —like the light, it seemed to come from everywhere. It sounded like glass bells and bright strings and some kind of woodwind, with a low buzzy undercurrent of pipes, somewhere between a waltz and rave music, and my blood spiraled in time with it. It reached inside and tugged at me to join the graceful, spinning dancers, but no. Not now, not yet.

Intricately carved sideboards of polished, dark-red wood were laden with food: plump berries like burgundy and purple jewels, mushrooms of all sizes, a mouthwatering rectangle of deep yellow butter, a delicately woven silver basket filled with speckled eggs.

Every legend says not to eat or drink in the faerie realm, or you'll not return for a hundred years. But my plan wasn't to return.

Still, food was the furthest thing from my goal right now.

I had no idea, however, how to find my parents.

I should probably find someone in charge.

I took a deep breath and forced myself forward, skirting the edges between the gaiety of the dancers and the temptation of the food. No one spoke to me, although I received a few curious looks—like I'd experienced my entire life. Now, though, it wasn't because I didn't look like my parents, or because I didn't look exactly human. It was either because they didn't recognize me or because I wore strange clothing: jeans, purple Docs, black hoodie that I'd pulled down off my head when the air warmed during my descent.

In contrast, they wore loose garments that seemed to move of their own accord, in a way that meant I couldn't quite focus on them. Earth hues, but rich and vibrant, or watery pale colors like the tapestries, or jewel tones. They were adorned with jewelry—silver and gold and precious gems—or with ivy and flowers.

I came around the dancers to the center of the cavern, and there I found Gwyn ap Nudd, king of the faerie underworld, and his bride, Creiddylad, the eternal May queen. I knew their names from Cerys's books; had memorized everything about them.

They sat on thrones carved from the same wood as the sideboard, his with owls and stags, hers with flowers and vines. At their feet lounged white hounds, their ears tipped bloodred: the Cŵn Annwn, Gwyn's hunting dogs.

I'd never assumed or even hoped that my parents would be royalty—hadn't really ever cared. I just wanted to find *my* parents, and go *home*.

But now I knew with a startled certainty that the king and queen of faerie *were* my family, because sitting at Creiddylad's side was a girl who could only be Cerys and John's real daughter.

I'd found them.

I could barely breathe. I'd imagined this for years, and now I was speechless.

The queen spotted me first. She tapped her consort on the wrist and leaned forward, her gaze pinning me.

"We have a visitor in our midst. Welcome to my festival."

She *said* she welcomed me, but I felt as if I were on display as all three regarded me.

The king and queen had hair black as a moonless night and skin the color of moonlit shadows, and eyes like mine, dark brown as the deep soil. But where I was plain and stunted, they were beautiful, otherworldly.

Creiddylad held out her hand. She wore green leather gloves the color of new oak leaves. Foxglove bells dangled from the wide cuffs embroidered with purple and gold flowers.

I wasn't sure what I was supposed to do, so I touched her fingers and curtsied awkwardly.

When I rose, I said—maybe too brashly, but I couldn't keep it in any longer—"Don't you recognize me?"

They regarded me for a long moment, and then he said, "You have the look of the fae about you, but your scent is human."

"I'm fae, but I've lived in the human world all my life," I said.

Creiddylad arched a delicate eyebrow. "A *plentyn cael?*" she said. "My goodness. Your will to live must have been incredibly strong; *plentyn cael* normally don't survive past their first year."

It was something I'd considered myself. My theory was perhaps Cerys had some faerie blood in her, from generations past, so her milk had been enough sustenance for me early on.

But I had never thought of myself as strong. Stubborn, maybe, but that had grown from how I'd been treated. People had judged, and I'd grown a shell to deflect their judgments, a wall that had protected me from caring about how they felt.

That shell had cracked, disintegrated to dust as I descended into the fae realm. I was home, so I didn't need it anymore, and now I stood here, open and vulnerable and aching.

"But don't you recognize *me?*" I said. "I'm your *daughter.*"

At least I had the satisfaction of surprising them. They both sat back, just a fraction, and their eyes widened, also just a fraction.

Then Creiddylad smiled.

It wasn't the smile I'd wished to see all my life.

I'd dreamed of a joyous reunion, of the delight in my

parents' eyes when they saw me. I'd dreamed of being welcomed, embraced, accepted by my people for who I was.

Creiddylad's smile was at best indulgent; at worst, condescending.

"Dear girl," she said, "you're mistaken. *This* is our daughter." She waved a hand to indicate the girl on the smaller throne next to her.

The girl had Cerys's generous mouth, and John's dark blue eyes. Cerys's curves, John's height, and something in the way she held herself reminded me of both of them. Poised, confident, graceful.

They'd named her Poppy, "our little poppet," and it certainly fit her, the blond child they'd brought home from the hospital, far more than it ever did me.

Yet she lacked one important quality that set her far apart from her birth parents, and that seemed to be emotion. She regarded me with the same polite distance that the faerie king and queen did; I sensed no kindness, saw no compassion in her blue eyes.

She was missing Cerys's fervor when Cerys told the ancient stories, made them come alive, shone a light on the magic in them. She lacked John's joy of cooking and his passion when he painted.

"No," I said. "I'm your daughter. The one you exchanged for her."

I wanted to ask them why. I'd always wanted to ask them why—but then, I'd always believed the exchange had been to keep me safe, to protect me. Or that maybe it had all been a mistake, and they'd been unable to find me again. Or any of a hundred obvious reasons why they'd give up their precious, beloved child.

Now I didn't want to know the answer, because now I was scared it would be one I'd never considered.

"No," Gwyn said, a hint of impatience in his voice. "She is

whom we chose, and whom we raised, and who sits at our side."

The girl smiled, but there was nothing in her eyes but ice. I felt as though I'd swallowed another gallon of frigid water from the well. I had no doubt that if she perceived me as a threat, that ice would turn in a flash to malice.

"But…"

"You've shown great fortitude, making your way here," Creiddylad said. "For that, we commend you; few have the will to do so without our invitation. You are welcome to stay, to feast, to make merry with your kind. Eat and drink whatever you wish; take a token of beauty, if you so desire. Consider it our gift." She leaned back in her throne. "But make no claim to kinship, because there is no claim to be made."

The three of them rose as one and walked away, the hounds trailing at their heels.

I had been dismissed.

I was trembling, not from fear but disappointment, and even some anger.

They had treated me as if I was nothing more than a stray cat: I could make a home in the barn, or I could leave; it meant nothing to them either way.

I didn't get the sense their stolen daughter mattered much more to them. It seemed they had chosen her because they'd wanted a golden child, not because they had any great devotion to her.

In fact, the stories all said the fae—like gentlemen and Hollywood—had a fascination for blonds. I'd just never listened. Never wanted to believe that part of the tale.

They didn't want me, and had made that clear when they'd abandoned me in another child's crib.

Stupidly, I'd even thought the other girl—Cerys and John's real child, the one they'd named Poppy—would want to change places with me, would want to go home and meet her real parents. But unlike me, she'd clearly never wished for that.

I'd wanted her to go back, too, so that Cerys and John could have their real child back, and be truly happy.

The faerie king and queen had praised my strength. That strength, that stubbornness had come not from from them, but from Cerys and John. My will to live was something they'd imbued in me when they'd fought for my survival in that tenuous first year.

It had come from the love they'd given me, unconditionally, when they'd accepted me as their daughter. They hadn't wanted blond, stolen Poppy back any more than the faerie king and queen wanted me back.

Love. Acceptance. A home. All from them.

I'd wished all my life for a family I already had.

I was a sodding idiot. A sound bubbled out of me, half-sob, half-laugh, taking with it a painful weight in my chest, one I hadn't known was there until it was gone.

I had to get back before Cerys and John found my note.

I desperately *wanted* to go back.

I turned and pushed my way through the dancers, not caring about politeness or propriety. I ignored the food, the music, the gems and silver and gold. All of it felt cold, empty —beauty without passion, without emotion.

So different from the warm, cozy cottage I'd grown up in and the comforting embrace of parents who loved me.

My real mum and dad.

At the end of the cavern hung a silk tapestry depicting a stone staircase. I didn't remember coming past it, but when I brushed it aside, I saw that staircase, the one I'd come down.

I went back up the slick, worn stone steps, carefully. I wasn't sure I'd have the strength to pick myself up if I tripped and fell. My thighs burned from the long climb, my lungs aching from gulping in the cold air, my stomach in knots, my emotions in tatters.

When I emerged, I saw the sky had taken on a pale peach glow of dawn. I'd been gone longer than I realized.

Then a horrifying thought struck me, and I fumbled for my mobile. It took a moment for it to find a connection, and when it did, I let out a long breath of relief.

I hadn't been in faerie for a hundred years. Just a few hours. It was the morning of my sixteenth birthday.

The cottage would be warm. There would be presents, and a cake—my father had baked it last night before I snuck out, white with chocolate ganache frosting. My mum would hug me, tell me what a smart, beautiful, creative person I was becoming. This year, though, I'd let myself hear the love in her voice, and taste the emotion baked into that cake.

The wall I'd put up, the one that hadn't allowed me to see and feel and believe that they truly loved me, was gone forever.

I paused beneath the hawthorn, running my frozen fingers along the cold, whisper-fine silk of my offering, and silently gave my thanks.

Then I turned and headed across the farmer's sheep field towards home.

Towards *family*.

HEAVEN HAS EYES

*J*ust before I moved to Southern California with my dad, my grandmother took me aside.

"You be careful out there, Cassie," she said. "California's full of kooky people—freaks."

If only she knew I was a kooky person *and* a freak, at least in her estimation. I've got a chronic disease (which she and the rest of my family know about) and I'm a lesbian (which nobody in my family knows about).

And what would my grandmother think of me now, sitting on the floor of the Barnes & Noble in Huntington Beach with my best friend, half of the New Age book section scattered around us?

This research trip was Amy's idea. We'd been talking about Wicca since we met, and now we were looking up a spell to ensure she'd pass her geometry final. I didn't think this was what Wicca was supposed to be about. Wasn't it supposed to be a religion, a celebration of earth and nature? Not a way to pass a test without studying.

I think Amy was trying to rebel, but I wasn't sure what she was rebelling against. I thought her parents were pretty great. Okay, they worked long hours, but they still showed up to all her school functions and had Sunday dinners together and all that. She even said they were pretty decent. Me, I was the one who had stuff to rebel over. My parents splitting up, my dad moving me across the country in the middle of high school, my juvenile rheumatoid arthritis. For the most part, I was a good kid. I just had a little lying problem.

Because I got good grades, didn't do drugs, wasn't about to get pregnant, and only drank the occasional glass of wine or beer at home with my dad's okay, there wasn't a lot for me to lie about, and my lies were almost silly. They'd just become automatic.

For example, no matter where I was going, I told Dad something different. Today, I'd said I was staying late at school to work on a science project. Dad wouldn't have had a problem with me coming to the mall, so I had no reason to lie. I just did. If I was going to beach, I said I was going to Amy's. If I was going to Amy's, I said I'd be at the library. Maybe I wanted to see how far I could push things. Maybe I wanted to get caught. Or maybe I lied about inconsequential things because they just didn't matter.

Either way, I hadn't started lying until I moved to California. (My sexual preference was a sin of omission; not really anybody's business.) I guess it had become automatic after the first one. "You do understand why you have to go with your father, don't you, honey?" my mom had said. "I'm going to be traveling so much with my research…you need access to good, regular medical care, and there are some great facilities in Orange County."

"Of course," I'd said. "I don't mind." Of course, Mom, I don't mind having nowhere to fit in.

I absolutely lied about my arthritis. People thought I was weird enough already, because it was obvious I had *some* condition that often got me out of regular gym class, and so anytime anyone asked, I made up a different ailment. Every week I was like the poster child for a new chronic disease. Some of which I'd completely made up.

Thank goodness I'd found a friend in Amy. At least she made my "acting out" seem like small beans.

Amy had bleached her hair almost white, wore Victorian goth clothes with Doc Martens, and announced that as soon as she was old enough to legally do it, she would be changing her name to Maeve (or Medb, as she often spelled it) Windseeker. To me, "Windseeker" sounded Native American, not something that went with the name of a fabled Irish queen.

All of which was even sillier when you considered that she was Hispanic.

"So, my mom took me to Little Saigon yesterday when she went shopping for ingredients to try a new dish," Amy said as she flipped through *A Spellbook for Teens*. Her mother was a chef. "It was pretty cool. I think we could get lots of funky herbs for rituals in the market. I didn't have time to look at a lot, though. They might even have Eastern magickal tools."

Oh yes, and her spell-casting. Last week it had been a love spell on Mark Fernandez.

"One religion at a time, please," I said. She looked up at me, her mouth downturned. I laughed lightly, but even to my ears it sounded strained. She went back to reading.

I scanned the bookshelves, but they were still out of Starhawk's *Spiral Dance*. I'd heard that it was a good book, that it talked about the spiritual aspects of Wicca rather than the right color candle to light to make the quarterback ask you to the prom.

"Okay, what about this one?" Amy stabbed a finger at the page. "We need sage, which I've got, a yellow candle, string, and an athame." She pronounced it ah-*thame*.

"I think it's ath-*ah*-may," I said.

"Whatever," she said. "It doesn't matter."

"You should at least know how to pronounce the tools you're working with," I said, more sharply than I intended.

"What is it with you today?" she demanded. "You've turned into Miss Critical all of a sudden."

"I just think your time would be better served actually studying for the test, rather than pretending to be one of the sisters in 'Charmed'."

I regretted the words as soon as they flew out of my mouth. Why couldn't I lie when it was important?

"Well, if that's what you think, then I'll just go." I heard tears in Amy's voice. I reached out a hand, but she stood up, grabbed the book she'd been reading, and stomped away.

Great. I'd just pissed off my best friend. Practically my only friend in Westminster. I slowly picked up the books scattered on the floor and re-shelved them.

I rubbed my hands, massaging out an ache I hadn't realized I had until that moment. Maybe I could talk to her tomorrow at school.

But Amy didn't come to school the next day. I didn't think much of it at the time. I figured she'd panicked about the test. Either she thought the spell didn't work, or she hadn't found an athame, or something like that.

But then her mother called me that evening. I was heating the oven for a pizza—my dad would be working until late— and reading my English homework (Shakespeare, but when my dad asked, I'd said Dante).

Amy hadn't come home yet, her mom said. My voice shook when I said I hadn't seen her in school and didn't know where she was. I promised—sincerely—to call if I heard from her. My fingers felt cold as I hung up the phone.

What had she run off and done now? For a moment I feared that I'd been wrong about spells—that they really worked, and this one had backfired, and Amy had turned herself into a toad, or worse.

She'd been mad at me last night. I hoped she hadn't been mad enough to do something stupid. I remembered her talking about Little Saigon. Had she gone back there to find something she needed for her spell?

I called her cell phone, but got no answer. I left a message without much hope that she'd call back.

I turned off the oven and made a quick sandwich instead, replacing the spicy pizza sauce and pepperoni I'd craved with mayo and ham. I ate it as I left the house.

I didn't know a lot about Little Saigon. It was the Vietnamese section of the city of Westminster. Some of the kids in my school were from there, but I'd never talked to them about it. I guess I expected it to be a run-down strip mall with Vietnamese take-outs and shops with grinning plastic Buddhas in the grimy windows.

Was I ever wrong.

The bus dropped me off at the entrance, which was bordered by a massive archway. It was nearly dark, but I could tell that the curved and pointed ends were painted red and gold.

I felt a little disoriented. The décor was Asian, and the people walking around looked foreign, but they were dressed like Westerners and everyone seemed to speak English without much of an accent. I asked about the market and was pointed to a two-story building.

The place was cavernous inside, with a high vaulted ceiling and wide walkways between the various clean, bright stalls. I smelled cilantro and raw meat, and an incense I couldn't identify.

I was amazed something so *unique* was hiding in the middle of a nondiscriminate southern California city. How could I have never heard anything about it?

Because it was getting late, the shops were closing and the place was deserted of customers. I walked down every aisle, peering behind things and around corners. If I hadn't been so worried about Amy, I would have been captivated by the beauty and grace and exoticness. As it was, there was no sign of her; if she'd been here, she was long gone.

I checked my phone. Dammit. I'd left so many messages for Amy that I'd killed the battery.

I went back outside. It was full dark now, streetlights illuminating the area. A full fat moon rose in the east. I didn't know where else to look. I should have gone home, called Amy's mom and suggested that Amy might be wandering around here somewhere. But despite the ache in my hips and knees, I wasn't ready to give up just yet.

Sometimes I lied to myself about what I was capable of, too.

I wandered down a side street. It was darker here, but there was something bright at the end. I stepped out into a courtyard and stopped, struck.

There were rows and rows of statues, gleaming white and almost unnatural in the moon's light. A forest of statues, all of people—ancient Vietnamese people. I wondered if they represented their gods. Just as I'd known nothing about Little Saigon, I knew nothing about Vietnamese religion or mythology.

I confess I did forget about Amy, just a little bit, as I walked among the ranks of expressionless figures. I couldn't hear a sound—not the cars on the nearby roads, not voices, not birds or wind. Just the sense of my own heartbeat. I wasn't afraid. I was enthralled. This was a holy place, sacred like a church, but less oppressive. These may have been gods, or ancestors, or both. But they were a memory of the past, something important enough to remember.

That's what I wanted to find in Wicca, what Amy didn't seem to care about. The past, the memories. The need to connect.

Each row was on a higher step than the last, so when I got near the end, I was at the entrance to the building that stood at the top of the courtyard. Even in the dark I could make out the sharp lines of the pagoda-like structure, the glint of gold in the moonlight. Two fierce Oriental lions guarded the entrance. In the darkness, I could almost believe that they watched me as I approached.

The teak door was open.

It was the type of place Amy might have come. It looked mysterious and magickal. She would have entered looking for a talisman, a magic charm, an item of power.

I entered looking for her. What I didn't realize until later was that I was also seeking answers.

Inside was lit with dozens of flickering candles. They dazzled my eyes, making it impossible for me to see anything at first. The only sound was my breathing; the only feel the thump of my heart. The incense in the room—the same as in the market—made my eyes water, even though I liked the spicy scent. I stepped slowly, carefully, farther into the room. The blackness around the candles seemed to go on forever. Certainly with each step I expected to see a far wall, but then I was further in than I thought possible and I still hadn't found any walls at all.

I turned and looked behind me. The door was gone. In its place, I saw a mural of blue and green and red and silver, depicting four animals in an Asian style of art: a dragon, a turtle, a phoenix, and what almost looked like a unicorn.

I must have gotten turned around, I decided. The mural was on the back wall. I turned back around to find the door.

A dragon loomed out of the darkness at me. An Oriental dragon, with big fish-like eyes and red horns and two spurs hanging from the side of its mouth, like catfish whiskers.

The head was as big as my body.

I tried to scream, but my breath was gone as if I'd been punched in the stomach. I stepped back and banged into one of the low tables that held a group of candles. I caught the table before it fell and righted the candles, wincing as the sudden movement made pain flare in what seemed like every single one of my joints.

When I looked back up, the dragon was gone. In its place was an old Vietnamese man, smoking a pipe.

I blinked. The smell of whatever he was smoking was pungent; maybe it was some kind of hallucinogenic. Maybe he was responsible for Amy's disappearance, and I was going to be next. Sold into white slavery. Sacrificed in a weird death cult ritual. Sautéed with bean sprouts and soy sauce, and sprinkled with cilantro.

I'd come here to find Amy, though, and I was going to do my best to save us both.

The old man was nestled in a bunch of cushions on a dais. To my relief, I could see the wall behind him; at least I hadn't entered a boundary-less space.

"I'm sorry," I said, because I was, in fact, trespassing. "I didn't mean to just walk in. I'm looking for—"

"I know what you are looking for," the old man said placidly. He sucked on his pipe, and smoke curled out of his nostrils, making him look dragonish. Except that he was of normal size. "You are seeking Answers."

The way he said it, "answers" was capitalized. In a way, he was right. I was trying to make sense of things, trying to understand my place in the world, trying to figure out if

Wicca, or some form of paganism, was indeed the path I wanted to follow.

I felt the urge to sit on a pillow at his feet and ask him a thousand questions, because he would have answers to all of them. Cryptic answers, no doubt, but ones that would come back to me when I was ready to understand them.

"Actually, I'm looking for a friend of mine," I said. "Her name is Amy..."

"She is not here, but she is safe and well," the man said. He smiled, his face dissolving into grooved wrinkles. "It is good that you care so much for your friend."

"If she's not here, how do you know she's okay?" I asked.

He gestured with his pipe. A coil of smoke spiraled towards the ceiling I couldn't see. "*Troi co mat*," he said. "Heaven has eyes."

"Are you a god?"

"If I was, would you fear me, Cassandra?"

"Yes," I said, thinking it was a safe answer. After all, he knew my name...

He chuckled. "Again you lie. You fear me a little, but you don't fear the idea of gods. But that's the sort of lie that can save you. Maybe you should have lied to Amy."

"I'm not sure," I said. "I would have been lying in a way if I'd kept my mouth shut and gone along with her spell-casting. I just—I just couldn't keep quiet about it anymore."

"Rather like your namesake."

I knew the story of Greek Cassandra, who was fated to always tell the truth. The problem was, nobody believed her. Was that why I lied? Because I was afraid nobody would believe me if I told the truth?

Or that nobody would care?

"So is it better to lie, or better to tell the truth?" I asked.

He was silent long enough, puffing on his pipe, that I finally figured out his point.

"I have to decide for myself, don't I? Great."

"We have a story about a buffalo boy named Cuoi," the man said. "It is said that he lied to Heaven, he lied to Earth, and he lied to himself."

"Why did he lie?" I asked.

The old man shrugged. "Ask him yourself. We know him as the boy in the full moon. He sits there under a banyan tree. The question is, of the three things he lied to, which one was the worst?"

He fell silent again, and this time I knew my interview was over. I looked around. The door was behind me, as it probably always had been.

At the doorway, I looked back, but all I could see was flickering candlelight. And maybe, just maybe, the faint outline of a looming dragon.

It wasn't easy finding a bus, and it was late when I got back home. My dad was in full-on panic mode. I realized I hadn't left him a note. He'd probably called my dead phone a million times.

"Where have you been?" he asked after he'd ensured I was all right.

It was on the tip of my tongue to say "at the mall," but I didn't. Instead, for once, I told the truth: "I was out looking for Amy. Her mom said she was missing."

"She came home," he said, and I felt happily weak-limbed. I flopped down on the sofa, chugged three Ibuprofen with my diet Coke.

Dad sat down on the sofa with me and continued. Amy had apparently run off with Gary Crenshaw, whom she'd had a crush on last year when he was a senior. Thankfully, she realized her mistake before anything bad happened, and went back home. I wondered if the love spell we'd done last week had really been for him and not Mark Fernandez. Or maybe it had all backfired.

Dad and I went through the whole worried/apology routine thing again.

"It's good that you care about your friends," he said, echoing the old Vietnamese man's words. "I know you weren't happy about getting dragged out here. I'm glad you made friends. It isn't easy, I know."

"Amy's kind of an idiot sometimes, but she's okay," I said, deliberately avoiding the rest of the subject. "Look, I've got to finish my homework."

"Dante, right?"

"Actually, it's Shakespeare." I paused. "Dad, you and Mom aren't ever getting back together, are you?"

He looked sad. "I'm afraid not, honey. It's not that we don't love you, or even that we don't like each other. It's just that we realized we want different things."

I nodded. It was the answer I'd been anticipating to the question I'd been too afraid to ask. Surprisingly, it hurt far less than I'd expected. I knew he was right; he wanted to settle into a home, and Mom needed her travel and research.

And I was somewhere in between.

"Thanks for being honest with me," I said.

Amy and I are friends again. I told her about going to Little Saigon to look for her, and she was pretty impressed. I didn't tell her about the old man, but when we went there together, I bought some of the incense and we looked inside the pagoda building. It had a few candles and Buddha statues, but it wasn't as big inside as I'd thought. Heaven may be all-seeing, but my own vision was still faulty. It was presumptuous of me to think I could see God, or the Goddess, or the difference between a dragon and an elderly Asian man, when I'd only just begun my search for understanding.

Amy and I have been talking more about Wicca as a religion rather than a fast fix. I think she's disappointed, but at least we're not fighting.

I also told her about my condition, and resolved to tell the truth if anyone else asked. Somehow, telling her made it feel more real to me, too; I had to be honest with myself.

I told my dad I was gay, and he hugged me and told me he loved me. That was it. I emailed my mom, and she said she loved me and supported me. I don't think it's any of my grandmother's business, though. But I won't lie if she asks.

I don't know why the buffalo boy Cuoi lied anymore than I know why I did. I'm working on it, though. And as for the old man's question, well, I'm not sure if there's an easy answer. It's not good to lie to yourself, but I'm still trying to figure out where I fit in the whole scheme of heaven and earth. All I know is that I'm a part of it. And that's a start.

*V*ery funny, guys."

I could still hear the other kids' laughter through my helmet comm as I tugged on the space station door they'd somehow wedged shut. Behind me, nothing but the vastness of dark and stars; Earth was on the other side of the station, the sun on the other side of Earth.

Then the giggling stopped, probably because they'd taken off their helmets. I was left alone with the rasp of my own breath and the insistent throb of my heartbeat in my eardrums, punctuated by looming silence of space. I was used to being alone; you'd think this wouldn't bother me.

It's one thing to be ignored, or to be called Doody Judy (seriously. As if we were all still in kindergarten). It's another to be locked outside in space.

I banged on the latch that was supposed to release the thick metal door. Nothing. Surely someone would come back and open it soon.

Right? "Guys, come on. Open the door."

My words went nowhere. Bile rose in my throat, burned my tongue, as it occurred to me that the bunch of stupid teenagers, my supposed peers, who'd never much liked me anyway, could just as easily forget what they'd done. Or not care.

On paper, to the adults, shipping kids off to space for school—the most remote prep schools you can imagine—made sense. It cut down on earth's overcrowding. More importantly, it was a closed, safe environment for us. There was nowhere to run off and play hooky. There was no way to obtain drugs or alcohol; any contraband would be caught in the entry scanners. We all—girls and boys alike—received birth control shots, so even if we fooled around, there'd be no unfortunate physical byproduct.

Adults have no understanding of how creative teenagers can be when they want to act out. We will always find a way.

In this case, turning on our grav boots and playing tag on the *outside* of the space station had seemed like a grand idea. Bouncing around on the white metal, dodging around antennae and solar panels and sensor arrays, surrounded by all that space—that was more fun that running around in the gymnasium.

Until everyone else decided to lock the one they didn't like outside.

Sweat trickled down my back, and my helmet filled with the stench of my perspiration, too strong for the air filters to handle. I pounded on the latch, and got nothing for my efforts but a sore fist. For safety's sake, the door doesn't lock from the outside, to keep one of us idiot teenagers from doing something radically stupid and getting ourselves killed. Which, given my predicament right now, made a certain amount of sense.

Oh, the inner door wouldn't release until the outer door was sealed and the compression was equalized, but that was automated and there were checks and triple-checks to ensure that never failed.

I stopped my efforts, clung to the handgrip beside the door, clumsy in my gloves, and closed my eyes. Tried to steady my breathing. I was scared to look to see how much oxygen I had left.

"It's not funny, guys," I said, hating how weak and thin my voice sounded. "Hello?"

If they'd taken off their helmets, I was talking to myself. Brianne had jammed the comm signal between our helmets and the staff's earpieces, so I couldn't even contact a teacher for help.

Of course, if I did that, I'd be a pariah. The truth of our out-station shenanigans would be revealed, everyone would be punished, and I'd be more of an outcast than I already was.

Shunning, or death. Some choice.

The mental calming exercises my therapist had taught me weren't really working, but I was able to step back from my panic just a tiny bit and look at the problem logically.

"Okay," I murmured aloud, which is what I always did when I had to work through a problem. (I'd learned to do it without sound, but that still looks like you're talking to yourself—see, e.g., outcast weird kid.) "Okay. They wouldn't let you die."

Would they? Honestly, I wouldn't place a bet on that. They wouldn't *mean* to, but they'd likely wait until the last minute, and any number of things could go wrong.

It was 2 a.m. ship time, thereabouts. Of course we'd snuck out at night. Brianne and James had rigged the sleeping quarters to indicate we were still inside, in case anyone checked the monitors. Like I said, never underestimate bored, creative teenagers—especially the cream of the crop, top of the intellectual heap.

Rise and shine was at seven a.m., with breakfast at eight and classes starting at nine. By then I'd definitely be noticed missing—maybe by breakfast—but by then I'd be a corpse stuck to the side of the space station by my gravity boots. Suits didn't carry that much oxygen.

"Okay," I said again, swallowing against the acid tickling my throat. Science wasn't my strongest subject, but we'd been given safety precautions, right? And I was far from stupid, even though right now my brain felt like oatmeal.

They'd jammed the door somehow. I just needed to figure out how to unjam it.

It took a few moments for me to pry open the case next to the door, the fat fingers of my glove making every motion slow and clumsy.

I stared at the computer panel until my vision blurred from tears of frustration and despair. I blinked hard, screwing up my face, willing myself not to voice the sob that rose in my throat. I was kidding myself: I had no idea what to do. Brianne and James were the computer geniuses. If that's how they'd jammed the door, I had no hope of figuring it out. If they'd jammed it physically, there was nothing I could do from out here.

Okay. Back to waiting it out. They weren't stupid. They wouldn't really let me die.

They wanted me to be afraid, and if I didn't give them what they wanted, it would stop being fun for them.

"Right, guys. Like I said, really funny. You got me. This is what I get for being the last one to go inside. Anytime you're ready, you can open the door. Can't say I've got all night, given my oxygen levels, but hey, I—"

That's when I knew.

That's when I felt it. The tightness in my chest, making it hard for me to choke air into my lungs. A prickling on the back of my neck, not from my hair stuck to the sweat there, but from the incontrovertible, primal knowledge, dredged up from some subconscious ability—

There was something behind me.

It didn't matter that there was no possible way anyone—anything—could be there. I just *knew*. Every nerve in my body screamed the truth at me.

I didn't turn my head and look. I couldn't. The muscles in my neck had locked down, pain flaring into the base of my skull as my jaw clenched shut.

My eyes squeezing shut, well, that was conscious on my part. If I didn't look, I wouldn't see...

No no no no no no...

There was no sound (there is no sound in space). There was nothing visible (I opened my eyes but kept them locked on the hatch, and with the sun behind the earth, there could be no shadow, and nothing crept around the limited peripheral vision my helmet provided). No smell, no taste, no touch, but fuck that, I *knew*, and my entire body seized up, waiting for something to happen, something to touch me or slither around in front of me.

I was breathing too fast—using up my air far too quickly, which panicked me more, and my face shield was fogging up, starting around my mouth and nose. Sweat dripped off my forehead into my eyes, stinging, blurring my vision, so that even if I wanted to look (which I didn't), I wasn't going to see anything anyway.

Which made it worse.

And that was when I lost my shit.

I begged and screamed and pleaded until I was hoarse, pounding on the door until my hand hurt so bad I couldn't stand it, but I still couldn't stop.

Apparently I sounded insane enough that they let me in, and when I still wouldn't stop screaming, the sound rough through my abraded vocal cords, even Brianne wasn't stupid enough not to find a responsible adult.

Although it turned out adults were the last thing I needed.

❀

Like the rest of the space station, Mr. Trask's small office was white. The theory was that anything reminding us of earth would make us homesick and maybe even claustrophobic, so there were no pictures of the ocean or photos of trees or even a nice potted plant anywhere. He had a small window, currently facing the stars as the hub slowly rotated, and shelves along two walls containing old printed books and a collection of antique little metal toy cars from, I don't know, a thousand years ago.

Over his head was an abstract print in blues and greens. I saw a tiger. Or maybe a tree. It might have been some kind of test.

While his own chair was ergonomic, not decorative, the chair across from it was slightly oversized and padded to the point that you felt as if you were sinking into it. I couldn't decide if the feeling was comforting or if it reminded me of being slowly eaten.

I resisted the urge to wrap my arms around myself. I hadn't been able to get warm, really warm, since being locked outside.

My right hand was in a splint; I'd broken a few delicate bones hitting the door. My voice was still hoarse, but my throat was healing after several days of not being allowed to talk.

Mr. Trask was long and thin, even his nose, as if he'd been stretched. I wondered if he didn't get enough exercise, which was crucial in space to prevent bone and muscle loss. I preferred Ms. Yang, my therapist back on earth, who had the benefit of being female and thus seemed to understand my problems more astutely. Mr. Trask seemed overwhelmed and distracted, which made me wonder how many of us he counseled.

Privacy laws meant he couldn't tell me, but if I had to guess? Probably all of us.

He smelled like garlic and basil, but then, probably so did I, and everyone else, because we'd had spaghetti Bolognese for lunch.

"Judith," he said, folding his hands on his lap and leaning forward slightly. "How are you feeling?"

I'd realized pretty quickly that the school's first priority was to cover its own ass. Making sure I was okay—and thus my parents wouldn't sue—was the primary objective.

I couldn't really fault that, honestly.

"I'm healing," I said, lifting my splinted hand. "Has anyone gone outside to check for…anything unusual?"

Mr. Trask tried to keep the expression out of his watery blue eyes, but he failed. I saw that annoyance.

"All the sensors have been checked and double-checked, Judith," he said.

"Sensors can be wrong," I said. "Or maybe what was out there doesn't register on our senses."

"Then it's not going to register for anyone who goes out there," he said, his voice level and reasonable. He paused, then said, "Judith, what you experienced isn't uncommon. Space amplifies agoraphobia—even for people who've never experience agoraphobia. It's perfectly normal that you panicked when you thought you were trapped outside."

After I woke up from behind sedated, I'd done my best to mitigate the damage to my reputation by insisting that my being locked outside was my own fault. I'd lagged behind, I said, and it wasn't anyone's fault to notice I hadn't been with them. And if the door had been jammed, it wasn't deliberate —or maybe I'd just overreacted and thought it was jammed.

We'd all gotten demerits for being out after curfew and being outside of the space station—including me—but nobody had gotten in trouble for anything more than that.

I'd seen relief on the face of every other kid who'd been out there with me, but they still shunned me.

At least they weren't making fun of me.

They wouldn't be making fun of me if they'd known what had happened to me out there. If they knew what was out there.

I reached for the clear plastic tumbler of water on the shelf next to me, took a sip to counteract the sudden dryness in my mouth, hoping my hand wasn't shaking, hoping the fact that I'd just broken out in sweat wasn't immediately obvious.

I wanted to go home, but I didn't want to go home. I didn't want to get on the shuttle back to earth, because the shuttle felt way more vulnerable than the station.

What I really wanted was people to believe me, but it was clear that if I didn't walk a fine line, I was going to get shipped home anyway. While medicated.

"I want to see the footage of when I was out there," I said.

"I don't think that's a good idea," Mr. Trask said. Now he frowned; my request had been unexpected. "It can only upset you…"

"No," I lied, against the pounding of my heart in my eardrums, "if I don't see anything, I'll feel better, won't I?"

But I didn't believe I wouldn't see anything.

And that scared the shit out of me.

In the end, the person who had the power to make the decision agreed. And I was back in Mr. Trask's office. We'd had tamales for lunch, and the scent of onions seemed trapped in my hair; I could smell it even though I'd pulled my hair back in a ponytail.

And it still felt cold in here.

His work station slid out from the wall; a horizontal desk from which rose an angled screen. He let me sit in his office chair so I could scoot closer.

I flinched when he stood behind me, and my voice shook a little when I asked him if he wouldn't mind sitting in the other chair.

"Are you sure you want to do this?" he asked.

"Yes." But the way his shadow had flickered across the screen, when he was out of my field of vision, made me feel sweaty and nervous.

I tapped the screen, flowed my fingers across it to start the video.

The camera was over the outer door. One by one I watched space-suited teens bounce their way beneath the camera, heading inside. Because the light came from the doorway beneath the camera and glinted off the helmets, it wasn't obvious who was who until a figure came into view and then the light went away.

I jumped back, startled, before my eyes adjusted to the pale glow of the lights dotted on the surface of the station. That final figure was me.

In the gloom, I saw my white-gloved hand come down on the door a couple of times, then pause. I saw my hand pry at the case over the panel next to the door, then pause again before slapping the case shut in slow motion.

Pauses, during which I thought about my predicament, or quietly asked to be let inside.

There was no sound with the video, for obvious reasons, but It reminded me how deafeningly quiet it had been out there, and now I heard my breath hiss through my teeth, heard my heartbeat, smelled my sweat again.

I wrapped my arms around myself now, from the cold and dread, and rocked back and forth a little as I watched myself panic. Watched myself banging against the door, putting my whole body into it. The fog crept up my face shield.

Suddenly, a flash of light, and I jerked back, blinking, before I realized it was the door opening and my body being pulled inside.

Then darkness again.

Mr. Trask stood and stretched an arm over to tap the video off.

"How do you feel?" he asked.

He didn't have to ask whether I'd seen anything, because he'd watched the video along with me.

There had been nothing outside with me.

Nothing visible, at least.

I stood in the compression chamber between the inner and outer doors, drawing in the stale, sterile air. Emergency suits hung in clear compartments set into the walls, five on each side. A row of lights arched from the middle of the chamber halfway up the wall, across the ceiling, to the other side, white and harsh. If I reached up, I could brush my fingers against the highest part of the curve; if I reached to either side, I could touch the suit compartments.

I'd left the inner door behind me open—I didn't have a suit on, and had no intention of decompressing the chamber.

I just wanted to... Well, I didn't know exactly what I wanted. To face my fear?

To decide whether something had really been out there, or whether I was going crazy?

It had taken me all day to psych myself up to even come here. Every step along the barren white corridors had felt as though the gravity had been increased tenfold. At the inner door, I'd stood for, I don't know, fifteen minutes? Half an hour? It had felt like days, just trying to convince myself to key in the code to open the door.

Stepping inside—stepping closer to the outer door, and thus closer to the emptiness beyond—had taken even longer.

My breastbone ached from the pressure of my banging heart.

I moved, one slow, careful step at a time, to the outer door.

There was no window in it, and I suppose I was grateful for that.

I placed my palms against the metal door. It was cold, but no colder than my bones felt, even though my plain cotton shirt was damp and heavy and stinky with sweat. No matter how many showers I took now, I never felt clean.

I leaned my forehead against the door.

Maybe Mr. Trask had been right. I'd panicked, outside and alone. Space was vast and terrifying, and I wouldn't hardly have been the first person to feel overwhelmed by it.

I don't know how long I stood there, trying to convince myself.

I don't know how long I stood there, wanting to believe.

I don't know how I stood there before I felt the first vibration beneath my hands and head, and heard the muffled boom of impact, magnified by the small area of the chamber.

I jerked backwards.

Then, slowly, I reached out and put my hand back on the door.

The vibration traveled through me; I felt it all the way to the soles of my feet.

Bang. Bang. Bang.

Someone—something—was pounding on the door to the space station.

This time, it wasn't me.

HIDDEN TALENTS

Tilly sat forlornly on the low, whitewashed dock that extended just far enough out into the pond.

Her formerly pretty straw sun hat, the lavender one with the silk flowers, dripped.

She dripped.

Behind her, up the sloping garden lawn, loomed the disapproving bulk of Miss Rosina Wakenshaw's School for Talented Girls. Although inside the windows were tall and the rooms bright, right now the dark stone exterior matched Tilly's sullen mood.

Tomorrow, the graduating class of eight girls—of which Tilly was one—would leave on the journey to be presented before Her Majesty, where Her Majesty would be told of each girl's Talent.

Which Tilly alone did not have.

Oh, she'd tested well when she'd arrived, showed all sorts of magical ability, mastered all the basics. But every magic user eventually showed a clear, specific Talent for *something*. A Talent clarified what the girl would do with her life.

Weatherworking. Animal communication. Herbology.

"Tilly!"

She didn't have to turn around to recognize the voice of her best friend, Gwendolyn. Gwendolyn's Talent was healing, although she hadn't decided where to go after graduation. Tilly knew Gwendolyn was putting off the decision in the hopes that Tilly's Talent would reveal itself, and they could somehow find posts close to one another.

"Tilly." Gwendolyn was somewhat breathless by the time she reached the pond. "My stars and garters, what happened to you?" She plopped down on the dock next to Tilly, heedless of her stockings or her Nile green day dress.

Tilly gestured. "My hat fell in the pond, and when I leaned out to get it, I fell in." She swore she'd properly pinned on her hat that morning, and the day was calm, not blustery, but there you had it. She brightened. "But look what I found: Miss Beaton's water-calling amulet." She pulled the amulet from her pocket. Miss Beaton had lost it during a water-casting spell she'd been teaching them. The aquamarine gem and gold links of the chain sparkled in the sunlight.

Gwendolyn sighed and plucked a water lily off Tilly's back. Tossing it back into the pond, she said, "Well, see, something good came of it. Although you won't be taking that dress on the trip. Which is why I've been looking for you —Miss Wakenshaw wants us to be packed tonight."

"It's ridiculous, Gwendolyn. There's no reason for me to go."

"No, *you're* being ridiculous," Gwendolyn said. Because she was Tilly's best friend, she was the only person Tilly would've allowed to say that. Except perhaps Miss Wakenshaw. She would've bit her tongue had the words come from Miss Wakenshaw. From Gwendolyn, though, Tilly knew they came from love.

"You're graduating along with the rest of us, so of course

you should come," Gwendolyn continued, as if they hadn't already had this argument.

They'd had it multiple times, in fact, and Tilly knew she was being sulky, knew this was just one last, futile effort. Without a clear Talent, she wouldn't be presented.

But of course she would go. She would go for Gwendolyn, to celebrate Gwendolyn's success.

She said as much to Gwendolyn.

Gwendolyn snorted. "If that must be your excuse, I'll accept it." She stood, flipping her long, honey-blond braid over her shoulder (she only wore her hair scandalously down at school; tomorrow she would be properly coiffed) and held out her hand. Tilly took it and stood. She wobbled slightly, but didn't fall back in. She jammed her sodden hat back on her head (her own hair, mouse-brown average like her lack of Talent, was in a short bob that skimmed the edges of scandalous—but everyone agreed it was safer that way, after the third time she'd set herself on fire) and allowed Gwendolyn to lead her up the lawn.

With each reluctant step, her wet stockings squished in her wet shoes.

She'd put them by the radiator tonight and with luck they'd be dry tomorrow.

With luck, perhaps Miss Wakenshaw and the other girls would all forget and leave without her.

Her shoes were not, in fact, dry the next morning, but Tilly simply had to make do. She pulled out the newspaper she'd stuffed in the toes and slipped her feet into them.

Her toes immediately felt cold and damp. Tilly wrinkled her nose, because a faint odor made her feel bad about anyone who might be sharing a car to the station with her. And anyone in the train car, for that matter.

Belatedly she realized she could have asked Miss Beaton to do a counterspell, but then she remembered Miss Beaton had already left for a sojourn in the Lake District.

She was shoving down the top of her overstuffed leather suitcase in the vain hope that it would close when Miss Wakenshaw came down the hallway, clapping her hands.

"Miss Rickart! Miss Smith! If we don't leave post haste, we'll miss our train."

As if Tilly wasn't ordinary enough, her last name was Smith. But, like her lack of Talent, there was nothing she could do about it.

"Coming!"

Tilly made it down to the front of the house. Footsteps crunched on the pale gravel of the drive as the school's manservant loaded cases onto the cars and the younger girls milled about saying their good-byes, their chatter tumbling over itself. Clouds had invaded the sky, but not heavy ones; the rain would hold off for another day or so.

Gwendolyn swung gracefully up into one of the two black Model-T's. Tilly put her foot on the running board, grasped the door, and attempted to do the same.

But her stockinged foot, now completely dampened, slid inside her damp shoe. With a sound less like a shriek and more like a resigned "Oh, bother," she fell backwards.

Thankfully for her, but not for him, their driver, Parker, cushioned her fall.

She sprang up, unharmed, with burning cheeks and babbled apologies.

But Parker, once he caught his breath, cocked his head and swore like a sailor.

"Parker! I must reprimand you for your language," Miss Wakenshaw said.

She was not a terribly tall woman, but she had a bearing that made her seem larger. She was quite pretty, Tilly thought, with strong features and eyes that missed nothing. Her aubergine traveling suit was impeccable.

As it turned out, however, Parker hadn't sworn because of Tilly's ignominious landing upon him, but because, in his prone position, he was able to see something wrong beneath the car.

"Begging your pardon, mum, but the pitman arm is loose. The nut's about to twist right off."

The pitman arm, it seemed, had something to do with the steering of the car.

By the time Parker returned with the necessary tool and tightened the nut, it was clear that they would miss their train, but it was better than having a breakdown halfway to the station—or, worse, an accident.

They were able to take the next train, though, and the trip passed without incident, although Tilly couldn't help but notice when Olive Gedge performed a good-luck charm.

Her cheeks burned. The other girls were her friends, too, but they had to consider their own futures. They understandably didn't want to miss being presented to Her Majesty.

She stared out the window, watching the rolling green countryside give way to factories and then the yellow brick buildings of the suburbs. The train rattled and shook, and even with the windows closed, she could smell the coal smoke.

Gwendolyn tried to engage her in conversation, but Tilly just didn't have the energy. A lady isn't supposed to sulk, and she tried to tell herself she wasn't sulking, but deep down, she knew she truly was.

Why had she met all the entrance criteria to Miss Wakenshaw's School if she wasn't anything special?

From the station they were whisked away to Miss Wakenshaw's London house, and after they'd freshened up and changed from traveling clothes to tea dresses, they went out for a proper luncheon.

The tea shop was crowded; even though all the patrons kept their voices properly hushed, there were enough conversations that the sounds seemed cacophonous. Tilly's head was bordering on the aching side of things, but she was hungry, and the tea sandwiches were marvelous. She couldn't decide whether the cucumber/dill/cream cheese or the cheddar and Branston Pickle were her favorite (although she took special care with the latter, because it often resulted in a stained dress).

As it turned out, it wasn't the Branston Pickle she should have been worried about.

The waitress came round to freshen their tea, pouring the aromatic Earl Grey into their china cups. The bergamot steam tickled Tilly's nose. She was feeling better now that she'd eaten something, and as such she'd joined the conversation. In a moment of unexpected animation, she'd flung her hand out to make a point, and as she drew back, her wrist collided with that fresh cup of tea.

When the hot tea hit her lap, she leapt to her feet, pushing back her chair.

Her chair collided with the gentleman standing directly behind her, who had been leaning over a woman at the next table.

The man cursed. The woman shrieked.

Tilly considered crawling under the table to hide from the mortification.

❧

"That was brilliant!" Gwendolyn kept repeating when they were back at Miss Wakenshaw's London house.

The shutters on the tall windows were pulled back to allow as much light as possible to enter the room, despite the grey clouds that were setting up shop in the sky. Mahogany bookcases lined the walls of the sitting room, which was dotted with slightly out-of-date furniture.

As much as she adored Gwendolyn, Tilly wished her friend would stop reminding her of what happened. She pressed her cool hands against her hot cheeks.

"No," she said, "it really wasn't."

"Yes, it was," Olive insisted, and the other girls hastened to agree.

It had transpired that the gentleman Tilly had bumped her chair into had not be a gentleman at all, not one whit. He'd been a *thief*, and he had just unclasped the woman's necklace when Tilly had struck him. However, the blow from the chair had made him drop the necklace down the woman's dress, and the police had been summoned.

But Tilly's favorite dress was probably permanently tea-stained, though, and *everyone* in the entire tea shop had looked at her, and it had been mortifying.

"Actually," Miss Wakenshaw said, entering the room, "Miss Richard is correct: it rather was brilliant."

All the girls stood and curtsied, then waited until Miss Wakenshaw indicated they should sit again.

"I have considered recent events," Miss Wakenshaw said, "and consulted with colleagues, and I am confident I have excellent news for you."

She took Tilly's hands, smiling. "Your Talent, Miss Smith, is so unusual, so unlike any we've seen before that we simply missed it."

Tilly felt her mouth drop open. She snapped it shut, but

hope and joy still surged through her. "I have a Talent?" she whispered.

"You do," Miss Wakenshaw said. "It's your clumsiness, dear girl."

Hope and joy trickled out of her as fast as they'd come. "Clumsiness?" she repeated. "But that's... How is that a Talent?"

"Your misfortune masks the good fortune that comes from whatever mishap you've had," Miss Wakenshaw said. "Think: you found Miss Beaton's amulet by falling into the pond. You saved us from having an accident with the car when you knocked Parker down. You prevented Lady Gedge from losing a family heirloom and helped put a notorious pickpocket in prison when you spilled your tea. Lady Gedge is extremely grateful, I might add, and will be making a generous donation to the school. So you also have my personal thanks, Miss Smith."

Tilly's mind wheeled and spun. She had a Talent after all.

But it was the most ridiculous Talent possible. It wasn't something impressively useful, such as truth-seeing or shooting or metal-working.

Her Talent was all about looking like a ninny. About never being able to have nice things.

"You're welcome, Miss Wakenshaw," she managed to say. "It's all...quite overwhelming. In fact, I feel my headache returning. If it's all right with you, I believe I'd like to rest in my room."

And she fled before the other girls could congratulate her. Later, when Gwendolyn came to the room they were sharing and expressed her joy, she thanked her best friend and accepted her hug, but couldn't bring herself to admit out loud how she felt.

Yes, she had a Talent. She wasn't ordinary.

Now she just felt like a joke.

Tilly had no excuse now, no way to protest being presented before the Queen. Her only hope was that Her Majesty wouldn't laugh.

The reception room was decorated with a Chinese theme, reds and golds and an ornate Oriental carpet. Tilly felt dazzled by the opulent splendor, although she tried to keep her attention on her own body so she didn't knock over a piece of priceless statuary or an irreplaceable lamp, or damage a piece of fine antique furniture. She glued her arms to her sides and stepped carefully.

There were more people in the room than she'd expected, too; she'd thought it would be just the Queen. Other dignitaries (Gwendolyn and Olive whispered names Tilly vaguely recognized), as well as others who were being presented for various reasons.

Finally the herald called for Miss Wakenshaw's School for Talented Girls, and Miss Wakenshaw led Tilly and Gwendolyn and the other six in a line to the front of the room, where Queen Mary, resplendent in a pale yellow gown trimmed with lace and a small diamond tiara, stood on a small dais. She was tall and stately, with dark hair and warm eyes.

"Your Majesty," Miss Wakenshaw said after executing a deep curtsey from which she rose without a wobble, "I am pleased to present the graduating class of 1923." She stepped to one side so Gwendolyn could step forward. "Miss Gwendolyn Rickart, whose Talent is healing."

Gwendolyn had tried to pull Tilly up front with her, but Tilly had slipped from her grasp and hidden at the end of the line.

Tilly swiftly realized the error of that: she had longer to contemplate her humiliation rather than getting it over with right away, longer to contemplate all the possible things that could go wrong, longer to…

It still came faster than she wanted it to.

"Miss Tilly Smith," Miss Wakenshaw said. "Her Talent… her Talent is one we've not encountered before, Your Majesty, and thus I'm unsure how best to name it."

Tilly froze, terrified, in her curtsy (not as deep as Miss Wakenshaw's or Olive's, but deeper than she'd expected of herself).

Perhaps Miss Wakenshaw wouldn't continue, would leave her statement there.

The Queen turned to look down on Tilly—even though Tilly was looking down, she knew, *knew* when the Queen's gaze struck her.

Tilly's thighs burned and shook, and she realized she had to rise up now or never be able to.

As she did, she heard Miss Wakenshaw do the thing Tilly had wished she wouldn't: Miss Wakenshaw continued.

"Perhaps the best word would be maladroi—"

And that was when the tip of Tilly's shoe caught in the hem of her gown, and to her mortification she stumbled forward.

A collective gasp sucked the oxygen out of the room.

Tilly caught herself, but the Queen was already stepping back.

At the same time, a curious noise whisked through the sudden silence, like a breath of feathers.

Suddenly people were shouting and red-jacketed guards seemed to come out of nowhere to surround and protect the Queen. In the melee, someone ran into Tilly, and this time Tilly did fall. She landed on her hand, felt a sickening pain shoot through her wrist.

As the edges of her sight dimmed, she thought, well, really, nothing could be more humiliating than this.

Once again, Tilly had been wrong. Because the next time she was brought before the Queen, it was also before King George V, and it was to thank her for saving the Queen's life. The poisoned dart had missed her only because of Tilly's stumble.

The assailant had, thankfully, been apprehended.

Someone in the royal court had a Talent for helping people forget things they oughtn't have seen, so no one present at the reception would remember the assassination attempt.

Except for the Queen, Miss Wakenshaw, Tilly, and Gwendolyn, because Tilly had insisted Gwendolyn accompany her.

Afterwards, as they sat in the the royal car taking them to Miss Wakenshaw's London house, rain sluicing down the windows, Gwendolyn asked, "How is your wrist feeling?"

"Only a bit sore, thanks to you," Tilly said. Gwendolyn had used her healing Talent to mend the break.

Miss Wakenshaw wrapped her gloved hands around the handle of her umbrella and smiled. "You know, I always suspected you two would find a way to work together, somehow."

"Work together?" Tilly felt foolish for repeating her teacher's words. But she also felt a rush of hopefulness, and she clutched at Gwendolyn's hand when Gwendolyn's fingers twined with hers, clutching just as hard.

"Obviously," Miss Wakenshaw said. "The more you use your Talent, the more you're going to need Gwendolyn to patch you up afterwards.

"I *told* you it would all work out," Gwendolyn said, her green eyes sparkling with happiness.

Gwendolyn hadn't, in fact, ever said that, but Tilly knew she'd believed it.

Plus, she had no desire to correct her best friend.

Her Talent might be unusual, might be mortifyingly embarrassing at times, but it could go so far as to save lives.

Even better, it was hers, and hers alone.

She'd never feel ordinary again.

*I*f I didn't have such an aversion to group showers and scary women's prison wardens named Elsa, I would totally kill my parents right about now. I would beat them about the head and shoulders with my French horn.

Except I don't want to damage my French horn. Hm. Let me work on that plan.

They had to drag me to this hick town in the middle of nowhere, where in order to be in high school band, you had to be in *marching* band, too, performing at the football games everyone else cared about. That's how I ended up stomping in a prescribed pattern around the middle of a wet field of crushed grass while the trombone player behind me kept taking an extra step and nailing me right between my shoulder blades.

I don't think anyone in the metal bleachers even noticed us. (Peru Central School: Too cheap to have bleachers on both sides of the field.) Certainly they didn't make much of a noise until the short-skirted cheerleaders bounded onto the field as the band was leaving.

The school was apparently also too cheap to dry clean the

rented blue-and-white band uniforms, because mine smelled faintly of the last person to have worn it. The chin strap of the Marge-Simpson-hairdo hat dug into my chin.

Wooh. Go Indians. Rah.

I'm apparently the only person in this godforsaken school to bother to look up the fact that Peru-*really*-upstate New York is so named because the mountains in the area suggested that country to someone. Apparently that person had never *seen* the Andes, because no. Not even close. No llamas, for one thing. No brightly colored ponchos, for another.

There's very little color here in October, actually; even the famed flaming North Country leaves were muted and depressed under the lowering grey clouds. It might snow tonight. *Snow*! Jeezus.

You know what's on the Welcome to Peru website? Pictures of cows. And tractors. And old people crossing the street.

After safely stowing my French horn and hat in the band room, I returned to the game. The players, all hulked out in their gear, were trotting across the weird red track material that ran in an oval around the field to get to their starting positions. I just wanted a hot chocolate to warm me up before half-time, when we had to march again.

"Who are we playing against?" I asked Herman who, despite having lived here his whole life (and his father is one of the janitors, because name your kid "Herman" and then *kick him while he's down*), cares even less about the game than I do.

Herman plays tenor sax. He's one of those guys who'll probably be quite attractive as an adult, but right now he has to suffer through scattered acne, spindly legs, and a kind of a pointy head. We kissed once, decided it wasn't going to work, and now he's pretty much my only friend here in hell.

It's not like I'm Prom Queen material, anyway.

He squinted, his breath coming in clouded puffs, and tucked his hands in his armpits. "Beekmantown, I think."

Beekmantown, which is apparently code for Impossibly Podunk Town. As if Peru is some kind of metropolis. In both places, people shove half a bathtub upright into their front yards to make little shrines. Seriously. Kill me now.

Kill me now was my last thought before we found the body under the bleachers.

An older guy (a live one, not the dead body) was down under there, too, in the soda-cup- and napkin- and condom-littered place, looking just as shocked. He had a camera around his neck, a battered silver flask in one hand, and a reporter's notebook sticking out of the multipocketed khaki vest he wore over a thick, dark green, wool fisherman's sweater.

Without moving from where I'd stopped, I rested a hand on the icy metal strut next to me and leaned closer for a better look at the body. Him, I recognized.

Male, mid-30s, slender build, wire-rimmed glasses. Brownish hair with bits of dead brown leaves sticking in the dried blood over his right ear.

Mr. Lundy, our English teacher.

Well, that sucked.

Beside me, Herman said, "Uh…should we do something?"

"No," I said. "He's dead."

"How do you know? I mean…."

Because dead bodies aren't like you see on TV, where a live person is playing dead. Even if the actor is stellar and doesn't twitch an eyelash, no matter how much makeup you pile on 'em, they still don't look really dead.

I'd been with my grandfather when he died. He was on palliative care, finally comfortable thanks to the morphine. When they say cancer eats away at you, they aren't kidding—

that's about as apt a description there is. Grandpa was sunken, the liver spots on his head visible now that his white hair was patchy and lank. His jaw had fallen open as he drifted asleep on the good drugs, as if he didn't have the energy to close it.

My dad had taken my mom down to the hospital cafeteria for coffee. I'd listened to her complaining about the hospital cafeteria coffee as they walked away, her voice and heel-clicks fading.

So I was holding Grandpa's hand—I swear he squeezed it once or twice that afternoon, even if never opened his eyes—and reminding him of the funny family story about the enormous ceramic ALF and the burnt-orange velour sofa, and I was laughing as I told it, and then I realized he was gone.

I think he wanted to know I was happy before he could let go. I think he wanted all of us to be happy, so I hope he didn't hear my mother complaining about the goddamn coffee.

But when I say he was gone, he was *gone*. What was on the bed was an empty shell. Not asleep; not really, really still. Just no longer there.

My parents came back and my mother said "Oh God" and my father said "I'll go get someone" in a whisper (because, why? to not disturb the dead body?) and I started to tear up and my mother said, "We'll cry when we get home."

And I thought, WTF is that all about? But I didn't cry. That's not what we do.

I didn't cry at the funeral, either, because they said not to.

Then I was never able to cry later, at home or anywhere.

The hospital room had resounded with silence. The metal bleachers overhead now thrummed with people stomping their feet and cheering. Apparently our team had done something good.

The older (live) guy—maybe in his forties? I don't know. I

couldn't see any salt-and-pepper hair under his brown knit pea cap—tucked his flask into one of the many pocket in his vest and started taking pictures.

"What the hell are you doing?" I demanded.

"I'm a reporter with the *Press-Republican*," he said, as if that made it okay.

He stepped closer and I said "Don't contaminate the crime scene!" Because yeah, I do watch those stupid forensic shows, even if you know that the person they're talking to at the ten-minute mark is the killer, and you can figure out by minute forty-three why and how he dunnit.

The older guy stepped back. He dug into yet another pocket and fished out his cell phone. "I'll call 911," he said.

Above us, the crowd roared again.

"This is really going to piss everyone off," I commented. "Because I think we're winning."

The police kept us there forever, asking questions. I was torn between wishing I'd been able to get another hot chocolate, because I was freezing, or being glad that I hadn't, because I really had to pee.

At least I hadn't had to march in the now-cancelled half-time show. I'll take my blessings where I can find them.

As soon as they released us, I made a beeline for a Porta-Potty. I'd've rather waited until I got home, but that wasn't going to happen.

My parents stood *rightoutside*. They'd had to be there while I was questioned, and now they were sticking to me like gum on the bottom of my shoe.

Unfortunately, this meant that I could hear them.

"I wish she hadn't had to see that," my mother fretted.

I had told them I was fine, but of course they hadn't listened.

"I wonder what happened," she went on.

"Well, wasn't he one of the...you know...them?" my father said.

"Oh, right," my mother said.

Holy shit. I felt like the top of my head was going to blow off and explode the Porta-Potty. Mr. Lundy was dead and all they cared about was that he was gay? And were they assuming that's why he was dead?

I wanted to shout at them for being so ignorant, but we just didn't talk about these things. I knew they'd ignore me. So I just growled under my breath, shoved my earbuds in my ears, and played Holst's "The Planets: Jupiter" really loud all the way home.

Loud is, after all, the only way to listen to "Jupiter."

Except my hands did start shaking, once we were in the truck. Yes, we own a dark grey Ford; apparently it's the law in the North Country that you have to own a truck. Because we had to get firewood and take our own trash to the dump. The dump where, on summer evenings, I am not kidding, it's a pastime to sit and watch the black bears.

And my parents *chose* to move here.

Anyway, I started to think about Mr. Lundy, and a part of my brain thought, hm, this is what delayed shock must feel like, because I couldn't get my hands to stop shaking and "Jupiter" sounded even louder than I'd set it, and the back of my mom's headrest, with the little tear where my dad had caught it with something, seemed especially in focus.

It's not like I'd known Mr. Lundy very well or anything. He'd been my teacher. But he'd been nice, in that way some adults are nice to teenagers, treating those of us with brains like we *have* brains.

Once he'd figured out that I actually *liked* to read (and

read something other than *Twilight*. Please.), he started recommending books. *The Princess Bride* (far superior to the movie). *The Last Unicorn*. Anything by Neil Gaiman.

Mr. Lundy's chin had been a little weak, and he'd worn glasses, and had nondescript sandy brown hair, and I don't know whether he was gay or not. But I was pretty sure he didn't deserve to die.

The reporter guy called me the next day. His name was Joe Dashnaw and he was normally a sports reporter, although he had co-written the front-page story. I knew all this because although my parents tried to keep it away from me, it wasn't hard to find the morning's paper in the pile next to the kindling for the woodstove in the family room.

"I can't talk to you without my parents present," I told him, which he should've remembered from yesterday.

"Off the record," he said. "I'm just curious if your memories of the incident match mine."

Well, of course you are, you bonehead. If you hadn't been drinking....

But the police hadn't said we couldn't talk to each other, and I was bored, so I said okay.

I went into the family room, where my father was dozing in the tan recliner we'd bought for Grandpa a couple of years ago, before he got really sick. A golf game was on low, and my mother was leafing through a *Better Homes and Gardens*. She and my dad had had a fight about her huge stash of them and whether we were going to truck two decades' worth of them to Peru.

I think she won, and they're in the basement somewhere. She'll never go back through them, mark my words.

I told them I was going to walk to Stewarts for some ice cream.

My mom frowned, setting the magazine next to her on the black leather sofa. "I don't want you walking anywhere alone," she said.

"Okay," I said. "Herman will go with me."

That roused my dad. He lowered the foot rest of the recliner. The springs inside twanged.

"I'm not so sure you should be spending so much time with this Herman," he said.

Oh for crying out— "He's just a *friend*," I said.

"Oh, George, it's fine," my mother said.

As if my mother would even know if we were doing it. She once said she didn't understand the purpose of premarital sex. And that, my friends, was the entirety of conversations we've had about the matter.

I was already texting Herman, and fifteen minutes later he showed up on my doorstep, and off we went.

It's probably stupid to out for ice cream in October, but it felt warmer today because the sun was actually out, and ice cream is ice cream after all.

Stewart's Shops were unique to upstate New York. The chain sold gas and some basic groceries; there was some sort of Milk Club where if you bought ten cartons of milk, you got a free one. They still used index cards to keep track.

They also sold their own ice cream, in gallons or in cones or cups. Each shop had a couple of Formica tables. Mr. Dashnaw was sitting at one, and raised a hand when we entered.

I ordered Adirondack Bear Paw (vanilla, caramel, and cashew crunch) in a cup, because someday I'll escape this godforsaken place and I won't be able to have this ever again. Herman hesitated, and I knew it was because he didn't have the money. So I ordered him a Black Raspberry and told him he owed me one.

We slid onto the curved, hard orange bench across from Mr. Dashnaw. He had a cup of coffee cradled between his hands. He looked better today that he had yesterday. His eyes were brighter, somehow, and he just seemed less...rumpled.

"Do the police have any leads?" I asked, and realized I sounded like a bad cliché.

Mr. Dashnaw shook his head. "Not really. Autopsy said he was hit on the back of the head. You know, they say most people are killed by someone they know."

What did that mean? His partner? A closet gay-basher?

My hands started to shake again, and I stuffed them between my thighs, as if I were trying to warm them.

"I didn't see any footprints," Herman commented around a mouthful of ice cream.

The ground under the bleachers was patchy dead grass, hard-packed mud, and scattered trash. But I remembered when we walked under there that I'd been kicking at the clumps of grass, upturning them, and there had been other areas of fresher mud.

"I don't think he would've just been hanging out under there," I said. "Maybe he was dragged there."

"Didn't he jog on the track after school?" Herman asked. I turned and stared at him.

He shrugged. "Sometimes I stay late and my dad drives me home when he's done work."

Come to think of it, he *had* been wearing sweatpants and a hoodie and sneakers. That hadn't even occurred to me until now.

Mr. Dashnaw asked if we knew about Mr. Lundy's home life, which we didn't. We talked a little more and then he said, "Thanks, kids. This might be the break I need. I'm really sick of sports reporting."

And I thought, awesome. Someone's dead and it's a way to further your career? But of course I didn't say it aloud, except to Herman, on the way home.

When I got home, my mother said, "Mrs. Fessette said she saw you at Stewart's talking to that reporter."

Crap. I *suck* at lying. I always end up with a big goofy grin on my face. "Yeah, he was there," I said. Truth. "He's really a sports reporter." Also truth.

I thought about Mr. Lundy, dead, and I didn't smile.

"I just don't want him upsetting you," my mother said.

"I'm fine," I said. Okay, that was a lie. But it was the kind we told each other all the time.

I couldn't fall asleep that night, no matter what type of music I listened to: baroque, rock, country. Tears clung to the back of my throat, scraped the backs of my eyes. Maybe if I slammed my hand in a door, I'd be able to cry.

No, then I wouldn't be able to play French horn. Have to work on that plan, too.

Tuesday night was the viewing, at the Brown Funeral Home in Plattsburgh. The main part of it had been an old house, and they'd tacked an extra part on, or maybe extended to meet up with the carriage house, hard to tell. It was painted white, with a zig-zag stone-edged walkway for people who couldn't get up the stairs.

I guess a lot of old people go to funerals. Now there's a depressing thought.

Inside was slate-blue acanthus-leaf wallpaper and gilt-framed paintings and dark wood furniture. It smelled overwhelmingly of flowers, all the different scents jumbled up and cloying.

Mr. Lundy's partner wore a new-looking dark suit, but the toes of his loafers were scuffed, and his hair was messy. I realized I recognized him: he owned the only used bookstore in Plattsburgh, a tiny place jammed full of books, with a rickety staircase that I was always sure was going to come crashing down under my weight and that of the volumes stacked along the edges.

We shuffled through the line. I looked at Mr. Lundy in the coffin. He looked worse then when we'd found the body, I thought. Now he looked waxy, fake.

We got to Mr. Lundy's partner, and I realized I didn't know his name. His eyes were red around the edges, but he managed a smile when I told him Mr. Lundy had been my teacher and I would miss him. I wanted to tell him about the books he'd recommended, but I couldn't. It was like I was suddenly, stupidly shy. But I couldn't get the words out; they stuck with the tears in my throat.

My father shook his hand, his voice hearty, as it always was when he was uncomfortable. My mother simply descended into unflinchingly polite mode, overemphasizing to convey fake emotion.

I wanted to kick them in the shins.

My mouth was dry, so I took a bottle of water and stood off to the side with Herman, who'd ridden with us. His hair was slicked over and he looked uncomfortable in his dress pants, which were a little short, and white shirt.

I tried to drink, but had trouble swallowing.

The reception line dwindled, and Mr. Lundy's partner sat down in a corner with people he obviously knew well. I wanted to leave, but my parents were talking to the Fessettes, and when my mother gets talking, God help us. Eventually my father would get bored and start poking her in the waist with a finger to get her moving.

Mr. Lundy's partner covered his face with his hands, and I saw his shoulders shaking.

Something hurt, deep and sharp in my stomach. Not exactly like wanting to throw up, not like appendicitis. More like something cracking, breaking.

And that's when I cried. Not for me, because I hadn't known Mr. Lundy all that well, but for his partner. For his parents. For the people who loved him, because he was gone and they would never have him again.

Then I realized I was lying to myself. I was crying for them, but I was also crying for me—for Grandpa.

My mother hurried over and put her arm around me. "No, no," she said. "You're not supposed to be sad."

Which was a stupid thing to say, and it only made me cry harder. She started digging in her voluminous purse for a Kleenex, but I knew all about her scary, crumpled, holey Kleenexes, and I squirmed out of her grasp and reached around for the handy box nearby. Funeral homes clearly buy them in bulk at Sam's Club, and for good reason.

My father said, "Maybe it's time to go," and I said, "I have to go to the bathroom," and that made them happy because at least I wouldn't be making a public scene anymore.

Nobody spoke on the drive back to Peru, through the dark and the cold. Herman patted my hand, and I suddenly gripped his, glad for his touch.

No, not that way.

The police figured out that Mr. Lundy had been killed by a transient, a drug addict who'd approached him for money.

The guy had been living in the woods on the other side of all the sports fields, and that's where they found him.

The fact that he'd been so close to the school was some scary shit. I half-thought my parents were going to decide Peru wasn't any safer than anywhere else we'd lived, but we'd moved here for my father's job, and the guy had been passing through, apparently. Headed south, where it's not so freaking cold.

My parents don't say anything about me losing it at the funeral home. They're probably not going to like it when the essay I wrote about Mr. Lundy gets published in the *Press-Republican*, because I mention his partner. They're not going to like the fact that I've realized that I maybe have a crush on a girl.

But you know what? I can talk about it with somebody else.

Because life is too short not to cry and not to say what's in your heart.

GIRL WITH A MISSION

$\mathcal{I}$n my school, I'm known as The Fixer.

It's a stupid name, which says something not very kind about the average creativity of the student body.

I'd gotten the nickname after I helped my former-and-maybe-again best friend Charlotte, after Charlotte had fallen in with the popular crowd. The idiots had developed the world's stupidest party game, "Whose Hooters?" (and its counterpart, "Pick the Dick"), which involved photos of private parts. You know, what came down to child pornography for high school students, if they'd been caught. I used my computer acumen to make them believe the photos had been leaked to the Internet, and shut down the game.

Now they thought I was brilliant. If I cared, I could practically call myself popular-adjacent.

So when head cheerleader Tara Kildare sat down at my table in the lunch room, I wasn't exactly startled. Just vaguely annoyed.

It was nearly Christmas, which meant white lights wrapped around palm trees and fake pine greenery everywhere. The Santa Ana winds were blowing, the hot winds from hell that made your eyeballs ache. I wasn't much for girly stuff, but when the Santa Anas hit, I bathed in unscented body lotion.

Normally I ate at the tables outside, but the winds had driven me inside, where I huddled in the air conditioned lunch room, an unassuming expanse of a place filled with round tables that seated six, uncomfortable molded-plastic red chairs, and the surprisingly enticing scent of Salisbury steak. From past experience, I knew the mystery meat dish didn't live up to its aroma, and besides, nothing beat Chef Boyardi ravioli cold out of a can. To make my meal more healthy, I'd brought two homemade zucchini bars. Cream cheese frosting or no, they included vegetables, so they counted.

"Brittani," Tara said.

Yes, I hate my name, and especially the spelling of it, but my mother loves it and I can't hurt her feelings. "Tara."

When I'd been in seventh grade—a time when nobody looked their best, Tara had taken it upon herself to walk up to me one day with all the confidence of being one grade ahead of me, curl her lip in a sneer, and announce that I was ugly.

My parents aren't religious people, but they have a strong moral code. My mother espouses what she calls the Bill and Ted Philosophy: "Be excellent to each other." This is why, in seventh grade, I hadn't kicked Tara in the proverbial nuts. However, I also hadn't developed a witty repartee, so I'd just let her flounce off.

This right here was the first time she'd spoken to me in four years. And even now, I could tell she was judging me, as her pale blue eyes took in my auburn hair, which I'd plaited into to braids in deference to the heat.

Still, she reined in her impulse to make a snarky comment, sucked in a breath, and said, "I need your help."

Tara's long black hair was pulled back into a ponytail, which went well with her cheerleading uniform. But the royal blue knit top with the school logo swoosh in red and white seemed almost baggy on her, and her naturally pale skin had an unhealthy pallor. She was clearly under a lot of stress over something.

Declining her request based on a nasty comment made four years ago would be petty.

"Meet me in my office after school," I said. "Room M102, first door on your left. But remember, I don't change grades, provide tests, or make fake IDs."

Tara actually looked relieved. "Okay," she said. "Um, thanks."

Her gratitude, and the fact that she'd swallowed her pride to approach me, made me wonder just how bad things had to be for Tara to ask for my help. I'd find out soon enough.

Room M102 was the band practice room (M101 was orchestra), and the first door on the left lead to the anteroom where the loaner instruments for kids who couldn't afford their own were stored. Two walls were covered with cheap metal shelving, on which sat black cases with numbers scribbled on them with thick silver Sharpie. On the wall opposite the door was a rack for upright basses, cellos, and trombones.

The 40-watt fluorescent lights all worked on a good day, and the ceiling was low enough that my head almost grazed those lights. My fingers were crossed that at five-foot-eleven-and-three-quarters, I'd reached my final height. Unfortunately, I'm not coordinated enough for basketball nor twig-shaped enough to be a runway model, so thank goodness I have a computers- and math-oriented brain to fall back on.

The small room smelled of slightly rancid valve oil and something I'd rather not think too hard about.

The storage closet was used for assignations among the popular band crowd.

Yes, there was a popular band crowd. Playing a musical instrument looked good on a college application.

No, I had not partaken of the room in such a manner.

Tara was ten minutes late.

"Sorry," she said. "I've never been in this wing before."

Her college application clearly focused on other pursuits, and no one came to the Nerd Wing unless they had a music class or were in the audiovisual club or some other nonpopular afterschool hobby.

I'm enough of a nerd that I help tidy up after band practices so often that Mr. Wilke, the director, gave me a key.

I leaned back against the shelving, my hip near my own French horn, and said, "So, what's wrong?"

Whatever was going to come out of her mouth, what she said next was probably the last thing I was expecting.

"I've been accused of statutory rape."

"Wait. What? You've been…you've been raped?"

"No!" She looked at me as if I were an imbecile, which made me wonder if I have that look on my own face a lot, dealing with her crowd. "*I'm* being accused of statutory rape."

"Look, Tara, I don't get involved in things the police should be handling—"

"Please," she said. I saw the tears brimming in her eyes, and suddenly I knew how hard this must be for her. She looked like Charlotte for a moment, when Char had asked for help over the stupid party game.

"Give me the details," I said, "and then I'll decide."

Because of those weird birthday rules that determine when you can enter kindergarten, Tara was already eighteen, which made her an adult in the eyes of the law. The person she'd slept with was seventeen, and the sex was consensual. Not exactly icky. Like I said, even this storage closet had seen some things. Sex among high school students was far from unusual.

But the other person's parents were up in arms, and wanted to press charges.

I wasn't sure what I could do. Out of curiosity more than anything else, I asked, "Who's the other person?"

Tara looked away. Sank her teeth into an otherwise perfectly manicured cuticle and worried at it.

"Tara?"

Her eyes flicked back to me. "This is confidential, right?"

"Absolutely." And it was. I would never betray someone who'd confided in me.

Still she hesitated, shifting from foot to foot, the muscles in her thighs flexing, while I ran through a mental list of possibilities. Whom had I seen Tara dating? She wasn't someone I'd paid attention to, given any thought to—and we didn't exactly attend a lot of the same functions. Except maybe football games, because of marching band. Thank the gods that was over for the year.

"Tara?" I asked again.

"Chaya. Chaya Gardner." It came out of her in a rush, and she wouldn't meet my gaze.

Oh. Her hesitation became crystal clear.

I knew Chaya. She actually lived down the street from me, and we'd been friends as kids. Not as close as Charlotte and I, but we'd hung out in the way little kids do when they share a neighborhood park.

Not just as kids, really. I'd been to her birthday party last year, a pool party in their backyard, one of a couple dozen teens.

She was Cambodian, if I remembered correctly. Adopted by the Gardners as a baby, after their mission in Southeast

Asia. Her three older brothers were the natural-born children of Jill and Frank Gardner, and Chaya had once confided in me that she thought they'd adopted her rather than try for a girl.

I'd had no idea either Chaya or Tara was gay.

"Okay," I said. "I can see why you want to keep this a secret—"

"It's not that," Tara said, and now her pale blue eyes flashed with anger. "I'm not ashamed, and neither is she. It was private. Our close friends knew, but we didn't see the need to advertise our relationship."

They'd been dating for two years. I am clearly not as observant as I'd thought.

Tara laid out the next, now obvious, wrinkle in the problem. The devoutly Mormon Gardners not only had expected their precious baby girl to remain a virgin until marriage, they'd expected a traditional marriage.

Imagine their surprise when they walked in on said precious baby girl with her very female lover.

According to Tara, even though Chaya insisted to her parents that she was a willing participant, they were sure Tara had manipulated Chaya, and they were outraged enough to press charges. They'd met with an attorney, but hadn't gone to the police yet (unless they'd done so today). In the meantime, they'd yanked Chaya out of school.

"Jesus, Tara, I'm so sorry," I said, and I was.

I mean, my parents had no problem with my being a lesbian, and even though we hadn't discussed it, I was pretty sure they knew my sleepovers with my friend Zan weren't platonic. At least nobody had to worry about an accidental pregnancy, you know?

"But I'm not sure what I can do to help," I went on. "Chaya's a minor in the eyes of the law, so it's your word against her parents.'"

"Chaya says her parents like you," Tara said. She was twisting a silver puzzle ring around and around on her forefinger. Because she'd lost weight, it was a little big. I'd bet money she'd gotten it from Chaya. "Maybe you could talk to them?"

Parents, in general, did like me. I was smart, polite, and didn't get into trouble. But did that mean I could convince the Gardners to back down from their religious wrath?

I doubted it. But I was willing to try. Tara might be judgmental and bitchy, but she didn't deserve this. And Chaya certainly didn't, either.

I dropped my backpack at home after school and walked a block over to the Gardner's house.

Most of the lawns in the neighborhood were green, in defiance of the drought. A few houses had gardens with native plants instead, succulents and rocks and a dry birdbath or a glass gazing ball on a plinth for decorative interest. The strong, dry winds had blown heavy palm fronds into the street, and I wished I'd grabbed a bottle of water before leaving the house.

The houses themselves were all two-story Mediterranean-style places with red clay tile roofs and stucco siding in some shade of beige, from pinkish-tan to yellowish. Some had brightly tiled entranceways, and most had black iron screen security doors, which allowed you to open the solid inner door and still have a locked door while you let the breeze in.

Not at this time of year, though. All the doors and windows were shut tight, with air conditioning keeping things cool inside.

Chaya herself opened the door, and she wasn't surprised to see me. Tara had texted her that I'd agreed to help.

"I'm so glad to see you!" she said, hugging me. Her dark brown hair was cut in a bob that accentuated her high cheekbones. But her hair looked lanky, as if she hadn't bothered to shower this morning. She was easily half a foot shorter than me, maybe a little more.

Her parents weren't home, but in truth, I'd wanted the chance to talk to Chaya alone, just to get her side of the story.

She led me into the living room to our right, two steps down onto a parquet floor covered with overstuffed furniture upholstered in Black Watch plaid. The vaulted ceiling had dark beams, and a fan in the center that turned at half-speed, keeping the cool air circulating.

The white-painted built-in bookshelves, credenza, and walls were covered with family photos, dating back at least a couple generations. Higher shelves held trophies of various sports.

Mrs. Gardner must have put spaghetti sauce in the slow cooker this morning, because the house smelled like garlic and tomatoes and basil, and my stomach rumbled. Ravioli had been a long time ago.

Thankfully, I'd brought chocolate-chip cookies as a peace offering—I'd been on a baking kick last night, and zucchini bread had been only part of it—so I helped myself to one now, while Chaya brought glasses of water from the kitchen.

"Thanks," I said, gulping down half of the water. I set it down on a sandstone coaster that bore a religious quote.

Chaya confirmed everything Tara had said, while fiddling with a silver puzzle ring on her thumb, confirming my suspicions.

"My parents are *furious*," she said. "I've tried and tried to talk to them…but they've never listened to me, you know?"

I knew. They'd dressed her in frilly pink dresses when she'd wanted to grub about in the sandbox; they'd sent her to ballet and tap lessons and she ditched them for Little League. She was smart, though, so thankfully everyone was happy when it came to school and grades and Student Council—they even stopped protesting about her playing soccer and field hockey.

"It'll be such a relief when I turn eighteen and can get to college," she said. "At least they aren't insisting I go out on a mission. They'd prefer I go to a local college, but I've gotten an early admission decision from UC Santa Barbara."

Far enough that she couldn't commute from home, at least, but a long enough drive that they weren't likely to drop in for a surprise visit too often.

"I feel sick to my stomach about Tara," Chaya went on. "I can't believe they're being so vindictive."

And the law, technically, was on their side.

I'd done a little research on my phone on the bus home. As I understood it, because of how close they were in age, Tara wouldn't be charged with more than a misdemeanor. But that could still mean up to a year in county jail...

Any fair judge wouldn't do more than slap Tara on the wrist.

Call me cynical, but I didn't have a lot of hope for a fair judge. Frank Gardner was a judge himself. He couldn't preside over the proceedings, of course, but he had friends.

I finished my cookie and my water, and got up to pace the room. Chaya followed me, pointing out people in the pictures. Almost all of them were in fancy, off-white shabby-chic frames that made my teeth itch.

The one of her parents in high school was kind of adorable in a parent kind of way. Mom had long, hugely curly blond hair and dark red matte lipstick. Dad wore a tux, but his hair was a shade longer than proper.

"Junior prom," Chaya said. "My parents were high school sweethearts—they'd been dating since eighth grade. Hypocritical, isn't it, that they think Tara and I aren't serious? I mean, yes, I know most high school romances don't last, and we're going to different colleges —if Tara even gets to go to college—so we could meet other people. But that doesn't mean I don't love her now."

There were a lot of photos of Chaya's three older brothers. I vaguely remembered them, all broad-shouldered and blond and sporty. They'd been a little bullying when I was a kid, but not in a truly mean way.

Hang on. In some of the photos, there were four boys. They all looked clearly related. Had Chaya had a brother who died? I didn't remember that, but then, it might be something the family didn't talk about.

"Who's this?" I asked.

"Oh, that's my Uncle Ted," she said. "My grandmother had a surprise kid later in life, you know? He spent summers with us, because he was just a few years older than Gary, my oldest brother."

Made sense. The Gardners weren't the polygamous type of Mormons, but they still had a large extended family. The backdrop of a lot of earlier photos—when Jill and Frank were younger, with their respective families, were clearly not taken in Southern California.

"Augusta, near Atlanta," Chaya said. "Mom and Dad moved here before Gary was born."

I heard the faint rumble of a garage door, and then a distant sound of a door opening.

"They're home," Chaya said, her voice tight with nerves.

Despite my own nerves, the Gardners seemed delighted to see me. Frank looked me up and down, called me a tall drink of water, pumped my hand once, and went off to his man cave or wherever. Jill sat on the edge of the sofa next to me and asked how I'd been.

Her hair was a darker blond, now, and cut in a ubiquitous middle-aged short style that still seemed too old for her. Her navy slacks and sleeveless ivory silk shell were timeless, as was the strand of fat rectangular gold chain links around her neck. She'd gained weight after three children, but she wore it well. Her fingers were heavy with gold and diamond rings.

I hate talking to parents, but I know how to pull it off. I said I'd applied to Stanford, among other universities, but that was my dream, and I wanted to major in computers. I mentioned the school's upcoming winter concert (band, orchestra, chorus). I asked about the market, because she was a real estate agent. I told her how delicious her sauce smelled, and she told me her secret was a tablespoon of brown sugar to cut the acidity of the tomatoes.

When we'd run out of chitchat (thank goodness—it was excruciating, except for the part about the brown sugar, which I filed away for later experimentation), she said, "It's so lovely to see you. You're such a good friend to Chaya."

The clear implication was, I was a good friend because I hadn't deflowered her precious little girl. I tried not to grind my teeth. I already have to wear a night guard.

"I know Chaya and I don't get the chance to hang out a lot," I said, "but she really is a friend."

"And she needs *real friends* right now," Mrs. Gardner said, reaching over and taking Chaya's hand in her own.

Chaya's back was stiff as a board, and I could tell she was doing everything in her power not to snatch her hand out from under her mother's.

"I agree," I said. "She's really stressed out—I'm sure you can see that. She's really worried about what's going to happen. Tara—"

At the very mention of Tara's name, Mrs. Gardner's

demeanor changed. Her back went as stiff as Chaya's, and any friendliness fled her face, replaced by a coldness that was kind of terrifying.

"Tara is no longer welcome here, and we will not speak of that *sinner* in our house," she nearly spat. "I think it's time you headed home, Brittani."

She stood, and I followed suit, feeling like I was a puppet with her strings being tugged.

I hugged Chaya, in part because it might piss off Mrs. Gardner, and headed out into the evening heat, mission definitely not accomplished.

My parents were due home from work soon, and it was taco night, which I'd helped prep last night, so dinner wasn't too far away. I poured myself a large glass of iced tea and made myself a plate of Wheat Thins and a hunk of sharp white cheddar anyway, and took it up to my rooms.

Because I'm an only child and our house is ridiculously big for three people, I have a second room attached to my bedroom, which I use as a place to study. Which was useful, because I have multiple computers and a lot of books, plus an electronic keyboard because I'm teaching myself piano. The bare spots on the walls not covered by shelves have posters of Steve Jobs and Bill Gates and Tesla and Einstein and Tony Stark. I have busts of Mozart and Wagner on one desk, and bobbleheads of all The Avengers on another.

I pulled my laptop from my backpack and flopped down lengthwise on the beat-up Victorian divan I'd found on Craigslist for a song (and attacked with a rented steam cleaner before I'd brought it into the house). My feet dangled over the edge, but it was still super-comfortable.

I had homework. I probably should practice my French horn.

But this problem with Tara and Chaya nagged at me.

No. Let's be honest. I was seriously pissed at the Gardners. And I wanted to find a way to keep this from ever getting to the legal system, which would likely screw Tara. She wasn't a friend, but there but for the grace of God, you know?

Plus, be excellent to each other. This wasn't *fair*.

I didn't know how much time we had until the Gardners officially brought charges against Tara. Even though the court stuff would drag on—I knew it wasn't like on TV, when cases get tried days rather than months or even years later— it would mess up Tara's life, and Chaya's.

I didn't open my laptop, because I couldn't even think why. Instead I dropped my head back against a pillow and closed my eyes.

Behind my eyelids I saw the Gardners' living room, looking like a family reunion had exploded.

It was kind of sweet, really. My family was tight, but small. I didn't have a buttload of cousins, a hovering bunch of doting aunts and uncles.

Like the Gardners, we didn't live close to relatives. My parents had ended up, independently, in the area for work, and met through friends. My closest relative was Nonna, my grandmother Lydia, in the Bay Area.

High school sweethearts, Chaya said her parents had been. Junior high, really.

I sat up so fast, I nearly dumped my laptop on the floor. Outside, dusk had fallen, and I could hear noise downstairs: Dad in the kitchen. He usually got home first, started prepping supper.

Was it reasonable to believe that Frank Gardner and his girlfriend, Jill (maiden name currently unknown) had taken and held to a purity pledge? As Mormon and devout as you wanna be, sometimes there's no denying raging teenage hormones, right?

I flopped back down. As if I had some Kilgrave-level psychic ability to induce them to admit they'd indulged in some serious hanky-panky back in the day.

Still, while I was lying there, I dug my phone out of my jeans pocket and texted Chaya: *What was your mother's maiden name?*

The answer came back almost immediately: *Zabriskie. Why?*

Just a hunch. Oh, and what school did they go to?

Hang on, I'll have to ask.

While I waited, I did my pre-Calc homework.

"Brit?" My mother's voice floated up the stairs. "Dinner, hon."

I went down, because *tacos*. My mother, not from a southwest state, uses store-bought crunchy taco shells and salty Velveeta and tasteless but tactile iceberg lettuce, but damn, it all works somehow.

I'd left my phone upstairs, because we have a rule about no cell phone at the table. When I returned, Chaya had responded.

Jackson High, Augusta.

I cracked my knuckles and called upon my Google-fu.

I found Frank Gardner. Graduated 1993. I found Jill Zabriskie, but no graduation date—her last yearbook photo was 1992, her junior year. I even found that prom photo.

I couldn't find a Jill Zabriskie graduating from any high school in the state that year.

Okay. It was time to go in deeper.

I paused long enough to do the rest of my homework—an outline of an English paper on a novel that changed my life (*The Last Unicorn*), Social Studies reading, Spanish worksheet.

My parents came in at some point and kissed me good-night and told me not to stay up too late, which they did every night. It was kind of comforting. I knew that if I truly wasn't getting enough sleep on a regular basis, they'd notice, and intervene.

At least, it made me feel good to believe that. It was hard for me to accept that Charlotte had been cutting herself, and her mother hadn't known. Char had finally confessed, and her mother had found her a good therapist, but still.

I went back to my research, after taking out my contacts and rubbing my tired eyes and getting more iced tea.

It was after midnight when I found a piece of information that blew everything out of the water.

I was at the Gardners' house bright and early, standing in front of the garage so when the door went up, I was blocking the two his-and-hers black Lexuses. (Lexi?)

"Brittani," Jill said. Today she wore black pants and a pale pink silk shell with a loose bow around the front. Same jewelry. She was like the cliché of a real estate agent, I swear. "I'm afraid I wasn't clear last night. You're not welcome here right now."

Frank, tall and burly, his mustache neatly trimmed and his cheeks red from his morning shave, made a point of looking at his watch. "I have to get to court, I'm afraid."

Fine.

"You'd rather hear this from me than see it plastered on the Internet," I said, my voice perky, a fake smile crossing my face.

"Brittani," Jill said again. "Yes, we'd be devastated if how Tara manipulated our innocent Chaya made the news. But it will soon; we can't stop that. Justice will prevail. It will only look bad for Tara."

"I'm not talking about that," I said. "I'm talking about your raging hypocrisy." Still with the smile. My cheeks hurt. Is this what televangelists felt all the time?

They both froze.

"What are you talking about?" Frank asked.

Suddenly, I could hear the Southern in his voice. In Jill's. Something they'd tried to erase. Tried to forget.

Just like this.

I waved a manila envelope. "Chaya's 'uncle' Ted. He's not her uncle, is he?"

Frank looked as though she'd sucked a lemon off the Meyer lemon tree in their backyard. Jill turned white and took a step back, leaning against her car. The look on her face made me almost feel sorry for her.

"He's your son," I persisted anyway, because I was pissed off, because she deserved to have the wound poked. "You got pregnant in high school, which is why you didn't graduate."

"Even if that were true—" Frank began.

It was true. Nice try, Mr. Gardner.

"What this means is that you weren't virgins when you got married, so how, exactly, can you insist that Chaya should be? At least she didn't get pregnant and have to drop out of school and pretend her child was her own mother's, and get her GED, and—"

"Jesus Christ," Frank said, which didn't sound very devout to me. "*Stop it*. Look what you're doing to her."

Rage bubbled up inside of me. "Look what you're doing to *Chaya*," I said. "You hypocrites. She didn't do anything you didn't do."

The front door opened. Chaya, with her backpack, headed for the bus. The bus I should be catching, too.

"What's going on?" she asked.

"She doesn't know," Jill hissed at me. "About Ted."

"Hi!" I waved at Chaya. To her parents, I said, "And I won't tell her, if you never bring charges against Tara. If you do bring charges, I'll post this all over the world." I tossed the manila envelope.

Jill caught it. I was impressed. I'd expected the high school football player to intercept.

"Those are just copies, obviously. I have digital files." I smiled, genuinely this time, and linked my arm with Chaya's. I bent down to kiss her on the cheek, because I knew just how much it would piss off her parents.

"I need to stop home to get my bag," I said, and Chaya, looking dazed, nodded. Just to her, I added, "Come on. Tara's waiting."

Fixed it. Damn, I'm good.

BEAUTIFUL BEAST

BEAUTIFUL BEAST

Teen pageant contestant Annabelle Moss sees her life shattered when her parents die in a car accident. A small ray of hope dawns when Gwendolyn Wentworth, the richest lady in town and former pageant queen, offers to take her in and be her coach.

Former child pageant contestant Taryn Wentworth hides behind oversized clothes and hair covering her face. At odds with her mother, she gives Annabelle the cold shoulder.

But as the world darkens and the real beast reveals itself, Annabelle and Taryn must rely on each other's love to survive.

A contemporary lesbian YA inspired by a classic fairy tale, Beautiful Beast *explores what it really means to be beautiful...and beloved.*

CHAPTER 1

The stage lights are blindingly hot, but my smile doesn't waver. My makeup doesn't melt. Around me, the other girls smell like too much perfume, too much nervousness; baby powder sweet and perspiration sour. All sounds seems heightened, from the blood pounding in my ears, to the tiny cough Charlene Carpenter almost suppresses, to the whine of the lead judge's microphone as he leans forward to speak.

To the sound of his voice, loud and clear, as he asks me the question that for so long, I feared the most.

"What is the biggest challenge you've had to overcome in your life?"

The stage lights mean I can't see past the judges. But I know who's out there. I can feel their eyes on me. I can feel their encouragement.

I can feel their love.

I take in a deep breath, as unobtrusively as I can, and never losing my smile, projecting confidence into my voice so it doesn't waver, not one tiny bit, I say,

"The biggest challenge I have faced in my life was when my parents died in a car accident when I was a junior in high school...."

CHAPTER 2

The gate outside the Wentworth house—no, I was going to have to revise my expectations and call it the Wentworth estate—was a large, black wrought iron affair between two heavy brick pillars. The gate design was of enormous roses, stems and leaves twining delicately through the uprights, which now split in half as the gates ponderously swung open in front of us.

I'd known the Wentworths were wealthy, but I hadn't imagined this. My family had been, I don't know, doing fine, before...before...

I sucked in a long, slow breath, forcing the tears back. My nose still felt swollen, tender from backed-up grief. I hadn't been sleeping well, and that made things worse.

In the sideview mirror, I watched the gates ease shut behind us.

Perfectly spaced trees lined both sides of the long drive-way. Beeches, I thought, but tree identification wasn't my strong suit. No matter what they were, I imagined they looked spectacular in autumn. Now, at the beginning of summer, bright green leaves pushed out into a bushy cluster.

They were all the same approximate shape and size, and in my exhaustion, made the driveway seem to go on and on, repeating endlessly, with the house at the end never seeming to get bigger.

Until bam, there it was, looming in front of us.

White against the green fields that surrounded it and the carefully trimmed hedges that bordered either side of the entranceway. Three stories, the top with dormer windows sticking out of the sloped grey-tiled roof. Big. Bigger than I'd expected, coming from a modest three-bedroom family home in town.

I'd said goodbye to that house this morning, forever.

This would be my new home for the next year or so, at least. I had no idea. It was hard to think beyond the next hour, the next moment. Grief, my counselor had told me, dicked with how we handled time. You stopped wanting to plan ahead, when all your plans had been shattered in an instant and the future was irrevocably changed, out of your control.

I liked my counselor. He hadn't pull punches. That had helped, a little.

Mrs. Wentworth—"But you can call me Gwendolyn, dear"—pulled up in front of the house (Mansion. Manor.), car tires crunching on the immaculate semicircle of pale pinky-beige gravel. "I'll pull the car into the garage later," she said, cutting the engine. "This way you get to see the house as it's meant to be seen."

I twisted around to grab my backpack from the back seat, then stepped out of the car. The summer air, heavy with the scent of cut grass, felt like a warm blanket on my bare arms after the air-conditioned car interior.

Four shallow, wide stone steps led up to the double front doors. I followed Mrs. Wentworth—I couldn't bring myself to call her Gwendolyn; I'd been taught to respect my elders—

up, and she opened the left-hand door and let me precede her through. Her heels clicked on the black-and-white diamond-patterned marble floor as she came in and shut the door behind her.

Back into air-conditioning again, or at least cooler air. A massive, round, dark wood table sat before me, topped with an urn of fresh-cut roses. Their sweet scent permeated the entryway, so thick you could taste it. The two-story entryway was dimmer than outside, despite the afternoon sun gleaming through the stained-glass transom window above the front door to shatter a rainbow on the floor. I couldn't see the back of the house. This place just seemed to go on and on.

I took off my sunglasses, tucked them on the top of my head. They'd helped hide the circles under my eyes, inner bruises against my pale skin that Mrs. Wentworth had tsked over when she'd picked me up today, taking my chin in her manicured hand and turning my head this way and that, her famous blue eyes studying me so long I fought not to squirm.

Gwendolyn Wentworth had been a beauty queen, celebrated on the pageant circuit, first runner-up in a major competition, before marrying and having a daughter, Taryn. She'd married well—better than I'd realized, apparently—but Mr. Wentworth was no longer in the picture. I wasn't clear on those details.

And now she was my guardian until I turned eighteen.

Annabelle Moss. Orphan.

My parents had been driving home on a rainy night when a driver who'd enjoyed himself a little too much at a St. Patrick's Day party plowed into them. They were killed instantly, a fact that was supposed to give me some comfort ("They didn't suffer"), but all it gave me was the sharp, sudden severance of my old life. Relatively happy high school junior to devastated orphan in one phone call.

Aunt Patricia, my mother's sister, had taken a leave of absence from teaching college in the city and moved into our house so I could finish out the school year. I somehow managed to keep my grades up. The school had let me make up tests, let me slide on some assignments since I was a straight-A student already, and I appreciated that. I was hoping for scholarships to get me to a good university. Fingers crossed for Ivy League, but I'd be more than fine with the next tier down.

But Aunt Pat had a job to get back to, and a one-bedroom, rent-controlled apartment she shared with her partner, Rhea. She'd been scouring rental listings every day, looking for a bigger place she could still afford on her and Rhea's salaries, and I was planning on a summer job to help out, when Gwendolyn Wentworth had swooped in like a fairy godmother and offered a solution.

I could live with her and Taryn, whom I vaguely knew from school. I'd be able to spend my last year of high school at the school I'd been going to all my life. She'd put me up, feed me, all that jazz, no strings attached. I had such a bright future, she said. She wanted to help.

And so, two days after the end of the semester, the paperwork had been signed, and here we were. My parents' house was on the market and Aunt Pat had gone back to the city, although from the way she'd hugged me goodbye, I'd wondered if she'd ever let me go.

Now we were pretty much the only family each other had.

I didn't really know Taryn at all, but I wondered if it would be like having a sister. I was an only child (I was nobody's child now), so I had no experience with that sort of thing. I had friends, but most of them had sort of…drifted away since my parents' accident. I suppose I'd stopped being much fun.

Fact was, I'd been so intent on getting through, on keeping my grades from plummeting, on surviving, that I hadn't had the energy for anything or anyone else.

Mrs. Wentworth led me through the downstairs, pointing out rooms: a powder room, the formal dining room, the formal living room, the music room, the den, another powder room, the solarium, the media room, the kitchen, the breakfast room, and I think a third powder room. There were back stairs (I wasn't sure if they were servant's stairs; I hadn't seen anyone else, but there was no way she kept this place clean on her own. Everything was sparkling, expensive, and immaculate. I was pretty sure I'd been able to see my reflection in the stainless steel refrigerator.), but she led me back to the rose-scented entryway so we could head to the second floor from there.

"Downstairs there's a pool and fitness room and sauna," she said.

There was a downstairs, too? I struggled to wrap my head around that.

"Everything is just beautiful, Mrs. Wentworth," I said. "You have an amazing house."

"Thank you, dear. It's so kind of you to say that."

"I think I need a map to find my away around, though," I added.

Her laugh was melodious. "You'll figure it out quickly," she said. "I know how smart you are, Annabelle." She added, more of a murmur, "And so pretty."

There was another reason, possibly the main reason, that Gwendolyn Wentworth had taken pity on me and scooped me up as a charity case to rescue. The former beauty queen wanted to share her knowledge and experience with me, because she saw my future (a future I was having trouble holding on to in my mind, but I was working on it) in pageants.

I'd done a few pageants as a child, and even though I'd loved it—the spotlight, the camaraderie, the attention—the family budget couldn't handle it. I'd done well enough, but we couldn't afford a top coach or expensive dresses or music lessons other than what the town offered on a sporadic basis. So I'd thrown my focus into school—math and computers were my passion, but I enjoyed science, too, especially the math-y parts—and saved my money from after-school and summer jobs, and I'd been headed for the county pageant this summer when, well, my world went to hell.

I'd had to back out of the county pageant, but Mrs. Wentworth was willing to be my patron, to teach me what I needed to know and buy the evening gowns and the makeup, and she was convinced we'd take the beauty competition world by storm.

It seemed unreal, the whole idea of it, right now. But it was also sort of a life raft that I clung to, something that would eventually give me a spark of hope.

Right now, I didn't have the energy to even think about it.

Two sets of stairs curved up, one on either side of the entryway, to meet at a balcony on the second floor. The balcony railing had the same rose pattern as the front gate.

We took the right-hand stairs. At the top, my sneakers sank into plush carpeting in a neutral cream hue. I wondered how it stayed so clean. Wide hallways stretched left and right. Mrs. Wentworth guided me to the right.

"Taryn?" she called. "We're home."

I heard shuffling, and from a doorway to the right, about halfway down the hall, Taryn Wentworth appeared.

She wore grey sweats and an oversized white T-shirt bearing artwork I didn't recognize. She was barefoot, and she held a book in her hand. As we approached, I saw it was a small black sketchbook. I'd forgotten until now that when I saw her at school, she often had one with her.

"Hey, Taryn," I said, raising a hand a little, not quite a wave.

"Hey," she said.

Everything had been so overwhelming—the drive, the house, all the details—and now, like an old movie where the picture fades away from the outside in, my world narrowed down to Taryn's face. It was all I could see.

Her brown eyes were barely visible beneath the bangs that half-obscured her face. Her drab-brown hair had been badly trimmed. Acne spotted her chin and the sides of her nose.

Most of all, though, I watched the parade of emotions that crossed her expression.

Pity. Resignation. A flicker of hope, although that one she managed to mask almost immediately, and I wondered what it meant. Or if I'd even seen it at all.

I searched for any sign of friendliness, of welcome, and found none.

I didn't blame her. I was an interloper, someone thrust into her life. I don't know whether her mother had discussed me with her, whether Taryn had had a choice or a vote in the matter.

Still, I felt a little piece inside of me curl up like a paper being eaten by a flame until there was nothing but a tiny pile of ash.

I needed a friend.

I wasn't going to find one in Taryn.

*

Beautiful Beast is available in ebook and print at your favorite bookseller.

ABOUT THE AUTHOR

Dayle A. Dermatis is the author or coauthor of many novels (including snarky urban fantasy *Ghosted* and YA lesbian romance *Beautiful Beast*) and more than a hundred short stories in multiple genres, appearing in such venues as *Fiction River, Alfred Hitchcock's Mystery Magazine,* and DAW Books.

Called the mastermind behind the Uncollected Anthology project, she also edits anthologies, and her own short fiction has been lauded in many year's best anthologies in erotica, mystery, and horaror.

She lives in a historic English-style cottage with a tangled and fae back garden, in the wild greenscapes of the Pacific Northwest. In her spare time she follows Styx around the country and travels the world, which inspires her writing.

She'd love to have you over for a virtual cup of tea or glass of wine at DayleDermatis.com, where you can also sign up for her newsletter and support her on Patreon.

I value honest feedback, and would love to hear your opinion in a review, if you're so inclined, on your favorite book retailer's site.

For more information:
www.dayledermatis.com

Written on the Coast: Thirteen Stories of Magic and Mayhem Written in Lincoln City, OR

NONFICTION

Researching History for Fantasy Writers: How to Use Historical Detail to Make Your Fantasy Worlds Rich and Compelling

Sign up for Dayle A. Dermatis's newsletter for *free* fiction, plus the latest news, releases, and more.

Sign up at DayleDermatis.com.

For more in-depth conversations and special sneak peeks, you can also support her continued work by joining her community of patrons out Dayle's Patreon.

Patreon.com/Dayle